Exquisite Interceptors

Cypress House Press
155 Cypress Street
Fort Bragg, CA 95437

Publisher's Cataloging in Publication

Yang, Thay.
    Exquisite interceptors / Thay Yang.
    p. cm.
    LCCN: 95-83332
    ISBN: 1-879384-27-2

    1. Paper airplanes. 2. Origami. 3. Aviation. I. Title.

TL778.Y36 1998   745.592
                             QBI95-20845

Cypress House would like to thank Marla Greenway and Marco McClean for helping bring this book to fruition. Thanks also to test pilot Mischa Reiber for valor above and beyond the call of homework.

First edition

2 4 6 8 10 9 7 5 3 1

Printed in the USA

Exquisite Interceptors

Thay Yang

Cypress House
Fort Bragg, California

Acknowledgments

I'd like to give special thanks to my mom and dad for their support; to my brother, Say Yang, for his great imagination and advice; and to my brother, Shue Yang, for his illustrations. Without their help, I would have been unable to complete this book.

Thay Yang

Introduction

Military planes are forever being updated and new versions conceived, but paper airplanes have remained simple and ordinary. Now, with this book, you can fold nearly exact replicas of sophisticated fighter jets like the F-5 Tiger, F-4 Phantom, and even the Stealth YF-23. You'll also find many beautiful, easy-to-make and fun-to-fly fantasy planes in this book, some modeled on sea creatures, insets and birds. These marvelous flying models are made possible as a result of the intriguing reverse fold and fuselage fold, which permits the sides of the plane to bend in special new ways. And the planes in this book, with their sweeping wings, working stabilizers, fins and air intakes, are each made of a single sheet of paper, without any cutting. You won't need scissors, just a piece of paper.

Thay Yang received recognition and compliments from the Museum of Flight in Seattle and from many paper-folding (origami) experts who read his earlier books. They inspired Thai to go even further with his paper airplane designs. This book is the result.

The planes you'll soon be making combine artistry and esthetic quality with agile performance. Using only paper and this book as a guide, you can create airplane models that are not only realistic and beautiful but fly faster and farther than any old-fashioned paper airplanes that lack the unique fuselage fold. The planes will inspire young and old alike to explore the mysteries of design and flight. You'll want to share your discoveries with your parents and your classmates (or your children, or design class). No matter a your age, you'll be delighted to create these wonderful planes and discover how well they really fly.

Folding paper airplanes has educated and excited people since the dawn of flight. Enthusiasts can learn a great deal about aeronautics while enjoying the challenge of learning to fold new and different airplanes that soar, dive, and zoom like real aircraft.

Thay Yang has always been inspired by things that fly. As a child, he remembers finding a feather from a wild bird.

"I looked at it and thought about it for hours. Then I launched the feather from the top of a hill and wondered as it glided smoothly down. I was so fascinated by it, I began experimenting with anything that might fly. I tried to throw leaves from different plants and trees, but they were too heavy to glide.

"Time went by, and I couldn't get anything to fly the way I wanted it to until one day in 1983 a teacher showed my class how to make paper airplanes. The folds and performance were so beautiful that I felt compelled to learn how to make different, better paper airplanes. I was amazed that paper airplanes could be accurately controlled and shaped in so many different ways. The possibilities are limitless."

Planes can be configured to fly in any direction by trimming the wings and tail fins. (See the Glossary on page iv for definitions of words. *Trimming* doesn't mean cutting. It means bending the trailing edge of a wing or fin to make the plane do terrific stunts.)

Some of the planes in *Exquisite Interceptors* fly like a dart, fast and straight. Some glide slowly. They are perfect for dogfights — try throwing a glider, then launch a fighter to intercept it in mid-air!

Paper airplanes are an endless source of fun, and you can make them anywhere, anytime. Thay is now 25 years old and engaged in "more serious" business, but the kid in him still enjoys making and flying paper airplanes. Age is no limit to those who wish to soar beyond the horizons.

Fold the planes in this book in the order presented, starting a new model only after you've mastered the one before. The techniques illustrated build on one another, so be patient and you'll enjoy the process, and soon control an impressive fleet.

You'll agree with Thay Yang that paper folding is challenging and rewarding.

Table of Contents

Practice Folds

The Fleet

Features

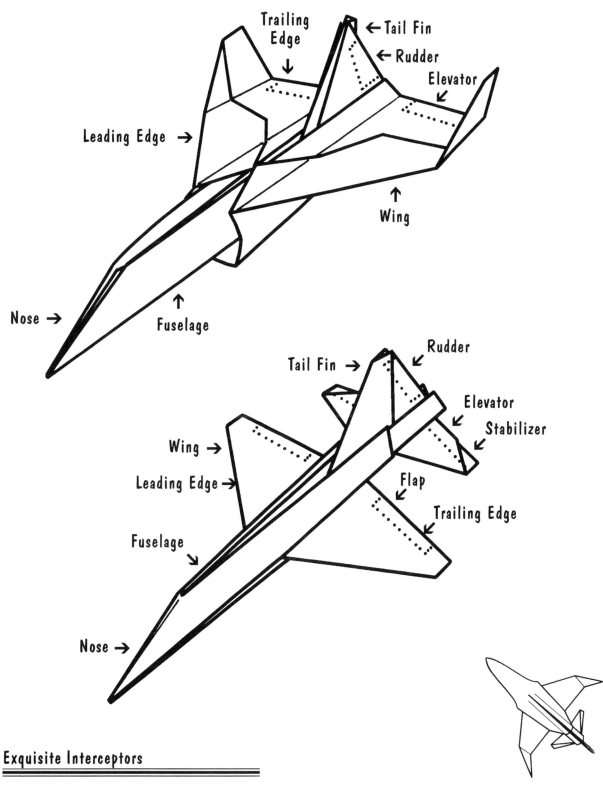

Trailing Edge

← Tail Fin

← Rudder

Elevator

Leading Edge →

Wing

Nose →

Fuselage

Rudder

Tail Fin →

Elevator

Stabilizer

Wing →

Leading Edge →

Flap

Trailing Edge

Fuselage

Nose →

Glossary

TRIM: Adjust by bending slightly.

DASH LINE: An imaginary line indicating where a fold is to be made.

CREASE LINE: A pre-existing line created by first folding, then unfolding.

FUSELAGE: The body of an airplane, housing for the pilot and engines.

WINGS: A pair of airfoils positioned on each side of an aircraft.

FIN: A fixed, vertical surface for directional stability of the aircraft.

STABILIZER: A fixed or adjustable airfoil designed to give longitudinal stability.

FLAPERON: An airfoil surface hinged to the wing and raised or lowered for lateral control.

ELEVATOR: A movable airfoil in the tail assembly, usually hinged to the stabilizer, to control a plane's up-and-down movement.

RUDDER: A vertically-hinged airfoil for turning an aircraft in flight.

DELTA WING: A triangular, swept-back wing.

NOSE: The front end of an aircraft.

THRUST: The force that pushes the aircraft forward.

DRAG: Air resistance that counteracts thrust.

LIFT: The force that pushes the wings of an aircraft upward.

STALL: A loss of airspeed that causes a plane to drop uncontrollably.

PIVOT POINT: A fixed point around which something turns (in this book, an identified point at one edge of a fold).

GRAVITY: The force that pulls objects down to earth.

Folding Hints

Before starting to fold any plane, study the symbols and signs on page 5 and 6, then practice the folds. This will prepare you for folding instructions for all planes. Master the practice folds before starting on any plane. Pay particular attention to the base folds, inside reverse folds and the fuselage fold. Refer to them later whenever you experience difficulty with the folding.

Every fold should be made firmly. Use the back of your thumbnail to press the crease. To sharpen the crease line on a base fold or an inside reverse fold (to make the crease hinge backward easily later), run your fingernail over it several times. Take your time on the inside reverse folds. They may seem like an awkward puzzle at first, but they will get easier with practice.

Making the fuselage is most important in finishing a plane. Work carefully, concentrate on the diagrams, and follow directions precisely. After you've mastered the inside reverse fold and the fuselage fold, the other folds will be easy.

Often when making a fold on one side, you'll do the same to the other side, back to back. This matching fold (or match-fold) makes both sides of the plane symmetrical, or even.

Each diagram shows the result of the previous step and leads to the next step. Looking ahead will help if you'd like to see what the fold leads to. The steps progress sequentially until the plane is finished.

For best results, fold each plane in sequence. You will need the simpler folding techniques that you will learn folding the first planes in this book in order to create the more complex planes found at the end.

The best paper is light 8^1/$_2$" x 11" copy or bond paper, although larger sheets of paper can also work well. Thick paper will not fold or fly well.

Find a flat surface on which to work, concentrate, and follow the instructions carefully.

After folding and flying these magnificent planes, you can experiment with various modifications. You may wish to change a plane's shape, combine different elements, or create entirely new airplanes. That's what Thay does. If you have patience and can let your imagination soar, you too can push the envelope of paper flight.

Flying Instructions

Before taking off, pilots always inspect their planes. Look down the nose of your plane to make sure the angles are symmetrical and not skewed. Straighten the wings and stabilizers on both sides, and make sure the tail fin isn't leaning to one side.

The first flight will test how your plane functions. Will it soar, or will it crash? If a properly made plane won't fly true, you may need to improve your flying skill. A well-made plane doesn't fly itself; you must throw it. The right way to throw a paper airplane is to hold the plane by its belly and throw it straight, using a steady motion and smooth follow-through after the plane's release. A glider must be released gently.

After the first flight, you may need to make adjustments to improve the plane's performance. If the plane nosedives, trim the elevator up to gain pitch stability and lift. The elevator is trimmed up and down by folding, not cutting. Keep adjusting until the plane flies straight for some distance, then glides smoothly down to a landing.

Each plane is different and requires a different angle on the elevator to balance the plane. Some planes need more trimming than others. A few require no trimming at all.

If trimming doesn't help, and if the plane has been properly made, then it may not have been thrown with sufficient force, or it may have been released

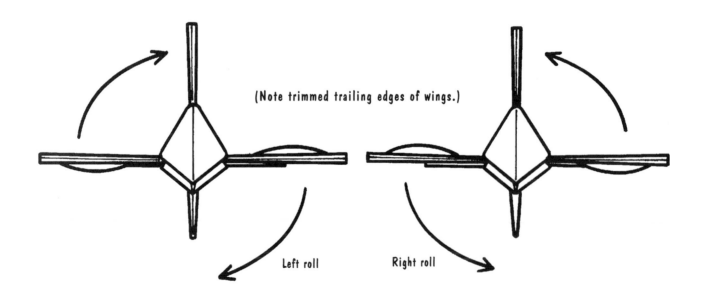

(Note trimmed trailing edges of wings.)

Left roll   Right roll

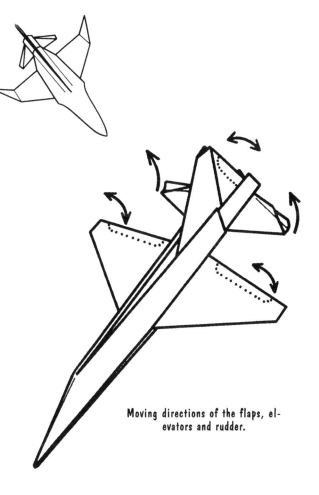

Moving directions of the flaps, elevators and rudder.

Study the plane parts and features on page *iii* until the names and locations of the flaps, stabilizers and other plane configurations are familiar. Familiarize yourself with the illustrations on page 2 which demonstrate how a plane rolls.

To perform a loop, trim the elevator upward and throw the plane at a 45-degree angle. The plane should make a loop and glide to a landing. If it doesn't loop, keep trimming up the elevator until it does. Trim the wings of the plane so that one side is up and the other side is down to make the plane spin as it flies.

Intercepting and crashing planes requires two paper airplanes. Throw the first plane high enough to smoothly glide back down. Then throw the second plane to intercept it. This game is much more fun when two or more players try to intercept each other's planes.

too soon or too late. Without sufficient forward thrust or timely release, the plane may dive or stall. Remember to throw the plane smoothly and at a constant speed.

If your plane does not fly straight, trim the rudder slightly on the side opposite the turning side. If the plane banks to the left, trim the rudder to the right; if it banks right, trim it to the left. The plane will usually fly straight if the fin is on center. If the plane spins or rolls during flight, adjust the plane by trimming the elevator or flaps opposite to the turn. When a plane rolls to the right side, trim up the flap or elevator on the left to balance the roll. On a roll to the left side, trim up the elevator or flap on the right side.

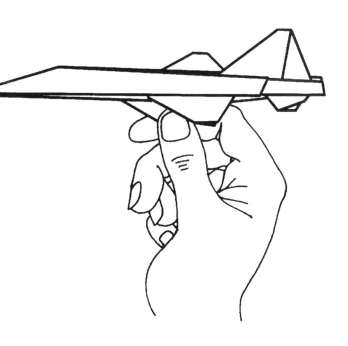

Holding position

Corrective Procedures

An airplane requires lift and thrust to fly. When a paper plane is thrown into the air, the act of throwing is the initial thrust. During flight, the plane gets lift from the wings, and the weight of the nose provides balance so gravity can pull the plane down and forward. The angle of the wings against the direction of flight deflects air downward, producing lift for the plane, so gravity actually helps the plane to keep flying.

The elevators control pitch stability and are located at the end of the tail section, usually on the stabilizers. To direct the nose up, or to level the flight, the elevator is bent upward to push the tail section down and raise the nose. The rudder on the tail fin controls the plane's directional stability (that is, it keeps the plane flying straight). If an air-plane is designed to be tight and aero-dynamic, it will glide smoothly through the air without being dragged to a stall.

When a plane is not properly balanced it will not fly well. When the nose is lighter than the tail section, the plane will not fly far. It will take off, then loop, drop, stall and crash. If this happens, increase the nose weight with tape. If this fails to correct the problem, the wings may be too big. Adjust this by refolding the wings to make them smaller. If your plane still doesn't fly well, make sure it is tightly folded and rigid. When a plane is loosely made, it tends to drag and may crash. In this case, bond the plane with tape at the back of the fuselage and under the tail fin. If it still doesn't work, trash the plane and make a new one. Back to the drawing board!

Should your plane bank to one side, the wings have probably come out of alignment. Hold the plane with the nose toward you, and check to see if one side is bent down or up. Adjust the wings so they are straight and of equal length on both sides. If this doesn't work, trim one side slightly, but be careful not to trim too much or your plane may bank the other way. It may nosedive if the nose is too heavy and the plane isn't receiving enough lift. Again, try trimming the el-evator up so the wings' greater angle into the wind can provide more lift.

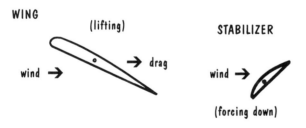

WING (lifting) / STABILIZER / wind → drag / wind → (forcing down)

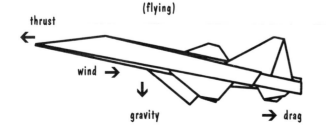

(flying) / thrust / wind → / gravity / drag

Symbols & Signs

1. Valley fold line
2. Mountain fold line
3. Crease line
4. Hidden fold line
5. Hidden edge line (will also be used to indicate a flap on a wing or elevators only).

6. Fold in direction of arrow

7. Fold towards the back, also called a backside fold.

8. Unfold in direction of arrow.

9. Fold and unfold.

10. Fold backwards and unfold.

11. Fold under an edge.

12. Flip model over

13. Push in

14. Parallel fold. Fold the new edge parallel to the existing edge as indicated by the symbol.

new edge   existing edge

15. Fold between these two points. Each point represents an edge line or a crease line.

16. This diagram shows the hidden fold line and edge line.

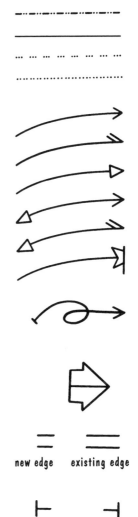

1. Tape.

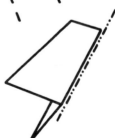

2. A picture of half a tape, like this, means tape here and wrap around to the back side.

3. Ruler, for measurement.

Perspectives

1. The valley fold is indicated by a simple dashed line. A valley fold pushes the newly created edge away from your face.

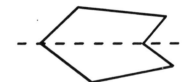

2. This diagram shows a mountain fold in the center and two valley folds on the sides. *Dashes with dots inside mean mountain fold.*

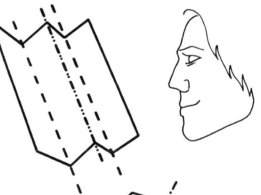

3. The mountain fold. A mountain fold pushes the newly created edge toward you.

Practice Folds

1. The Half Fold

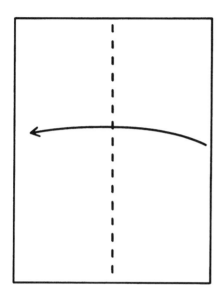

1. Fold the right side of the paper to the left side.

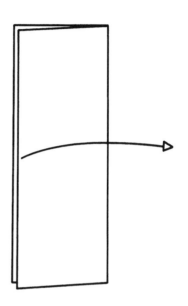

2. Unfold it to its previous position.

3. Finished fold with a crease line in the center. All the planes will start with a paper fold in half with a center crease line. Turn the paper sideways and fold it in half also.

2. Insert Under Fold

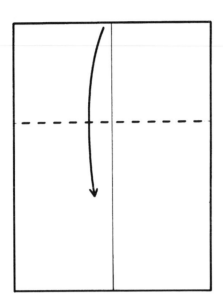

1. Fold your paper about ⅓ of the way down.

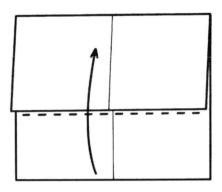

2. Fold the bottom half up along the edge.

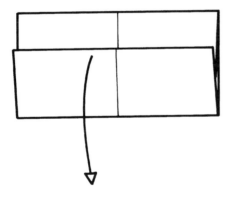

3. Unfold to its previous position.

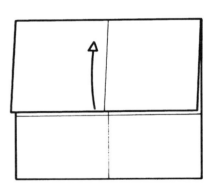

4. Lift the edge up.

5. Refold the bottom edge up under the top layer.

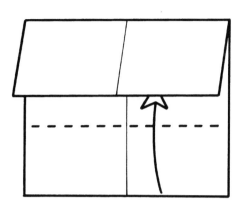

6. The folding diagram for "inserting under."

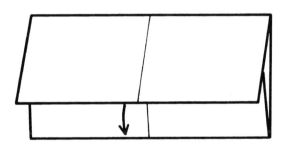

7. The completed "insert under" fold.

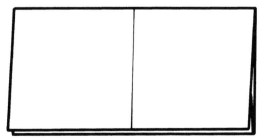

3. The Matching Fold

The matching fold is designed to even out both sides of the plane's fuselage, especially the wings, stabilizers and tail fins. This is a very important step for accurancy and performance. The wings need to be the same size and at the same position on the plane to balance it. *For this reason, the wings and stabilizers should be folded back-to-back every time.*

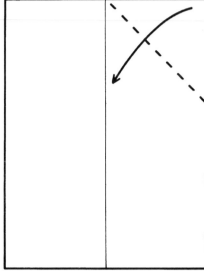

1. Fold the paper in half and then unfold. Fold the top right corner diagonally down to the middle crease line.

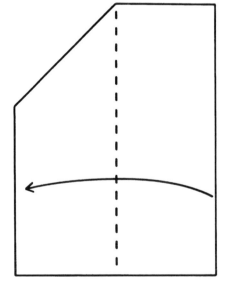

2. The fold should look like this. Turn the paper over.

3. Fold the right side to the left side.

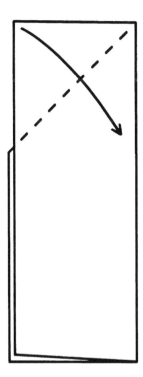

4. What you have now is a back-to-back position. Fold diagonally down to the right so it matches with the other side. Both sides should be even.

5. Match-fold the two left edges to the right edge on opposite directions.

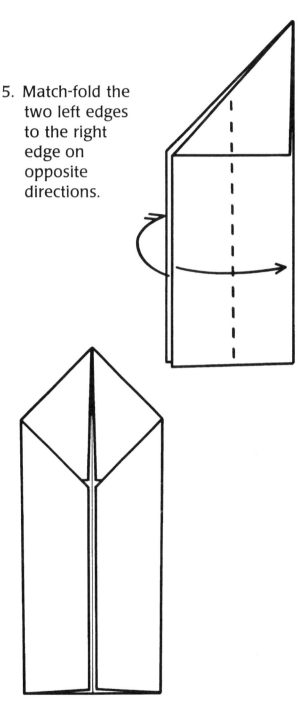

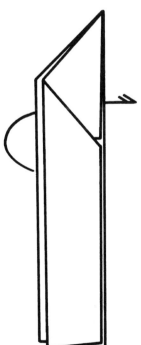

6. The matching folds are completed. Fold the back side to the right.

7. The matching fold technique gets both sides even as shown here. This technique will always be folded back to back and in opposite directions to the same point.

4. Inside Reverse Fold

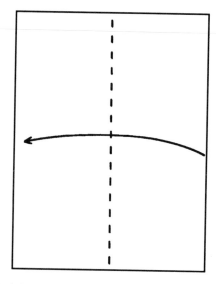

1. Fold the paper in half.

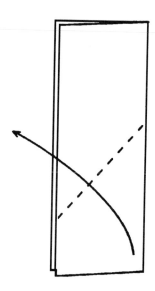

2. Fold the bottom half diagonally to the left side.

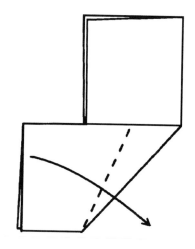

3. Fold diagonally back down.

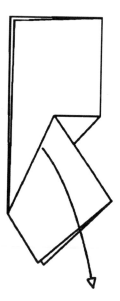

4. Unfold both folds.

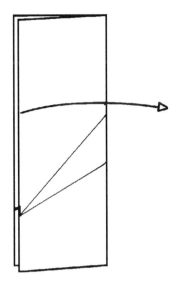

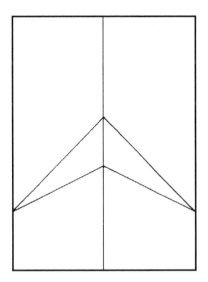

5. Open the paper out flat.

6. This is what the paper should look like with crease lines.

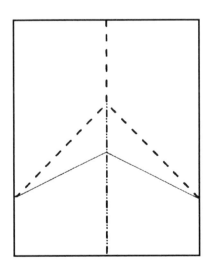

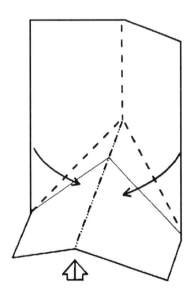

7. Use the top crease line for valley fold and the center half crease line for mountain fold.

8. Fold the two sides together and rise up the mountain fold line toward you as shown on this diagram.

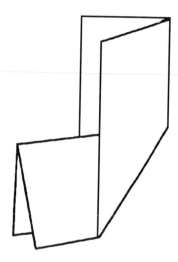

9. The fold looks like this.

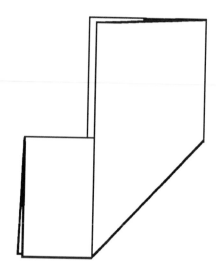

10. Push flat.

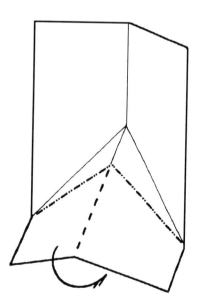

11. Open the paper halfway and mountain fold on the marked crease lines. (See page 4 for fold-direction signs.)

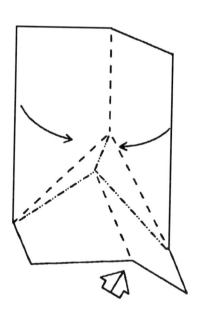

12. Fold the two sides of the paper together again with the bottom half of the paper valley folding away to the back side.

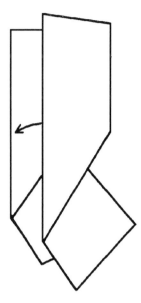

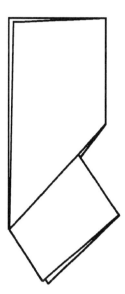

13. Close the paper tightly together.

14. Completion of inside reverse folds. This is a vital folding technique, so try it a few times before moving on.

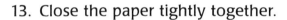

5. Triangle Inside Reverse

This is the same reverse fold technique as the previous fold, but it is more closely related to the shapes to come.

Practice until you feel confident enough with this shape and technique.

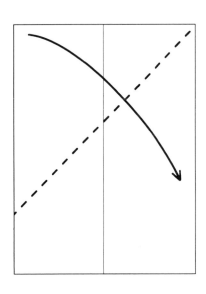

1. Fold the paper diagonally down to the right side.

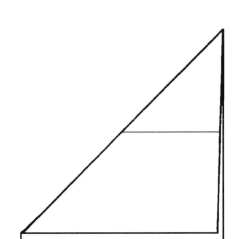

2. Diagram of the diagonal fold.

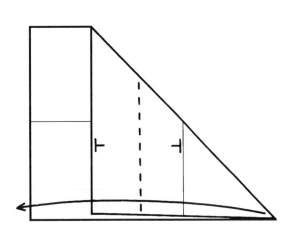

3. Fold to the left side between the edge line and the crease line.

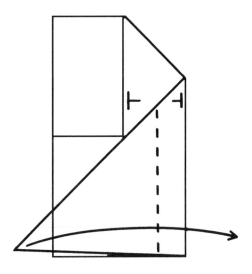

4. Fold the paper to the right between the points.

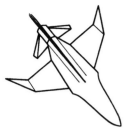

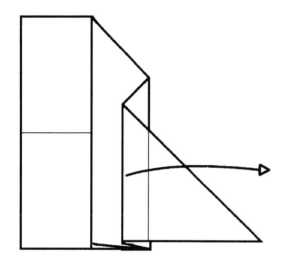

5. Unfold it to the right.

6. Lift the top layer up.

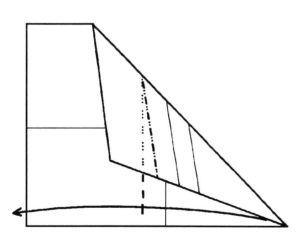

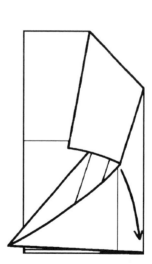

7. Make an inside reverse fold on the left crease.

8. The folding diagram.

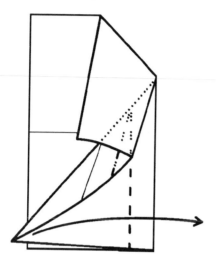

9. Make another inside reverse fold to the right.

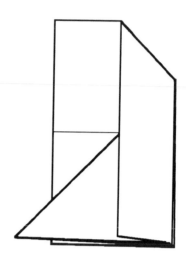

10. Completion of the first inside reverse fold.

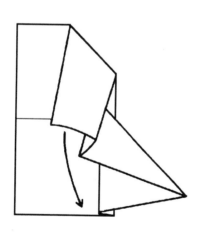

11. The folding diagram for the triangle inside reversal.

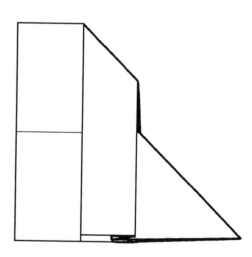

12. Completed triangle inside reversal.

6. Base Fold (1)

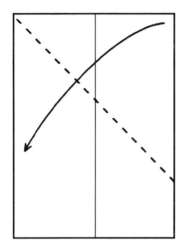

1. Fold the top right corner diagonally down to the left side.

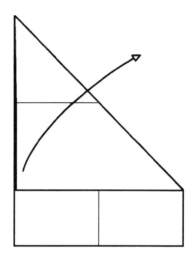

2. Unfold.

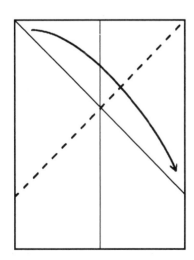

3. Fold the top left corner diagonally down to the right side.

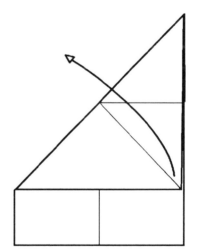

4. Unfold.

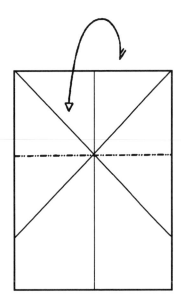

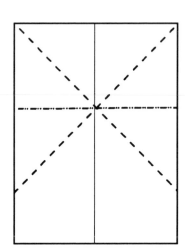

5. Mountain fold paper to the back on the center point, and then unfold it to the front.

6. Push the centerpoint of the creases in the paper with your finger to enhance the shape for folding.

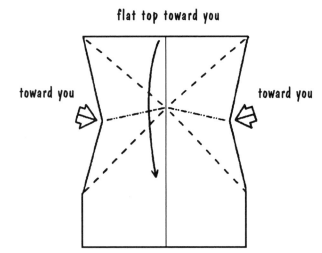

flat top toward you

toward you   toward you

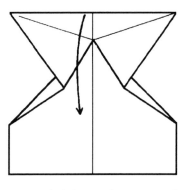

8. This is the folding diagram for the waterbomb base (1).

7. Create a water bomb by bringing the top edge down to the bottom with mountain crease lines folding in from the two sides.

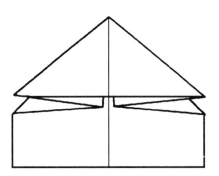

9. Base Fold #1 completed.

7. Base Fold (2)

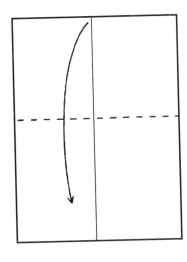

1. Fold the paper down 5 inches from the top edge. (This measurement must be exact; use the ruler on page 6 if a separate ruler is not available.)

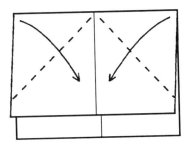

2. Fold the two top corners down to the center crease line.

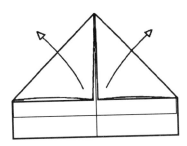

3. Unfold the paper completely.

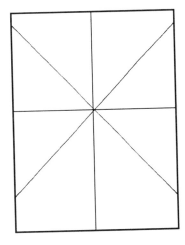

4. Turn the model over.

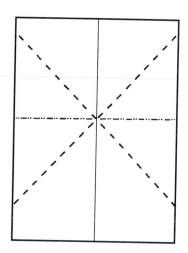

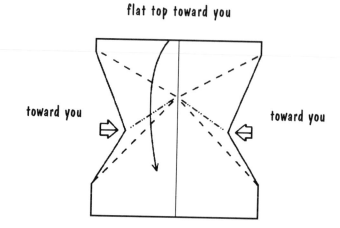

flat top toward you

toward you

toward you

5. Press the center point with your finger, and the paper will form a facile shape for the water bomb.

6. This is the folding diagram for the waterbomb base (2).

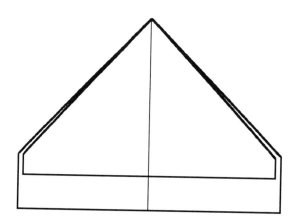

7. Base #2 completed.

8. Wing Fold & Pivot Point

This is a very important fold for the wing because it makes it the right size. This technique applies to the fuse-

lage and other folds as well. Start with a finished waterbomb (Base 1).

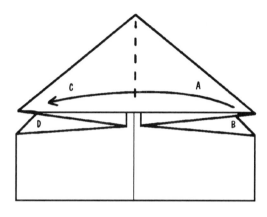

1. Fold flap A to the left side.

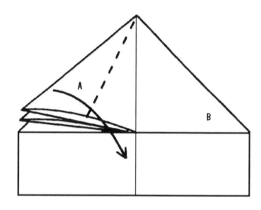

2. Fold flap A toward flap B, even with the center crease line.

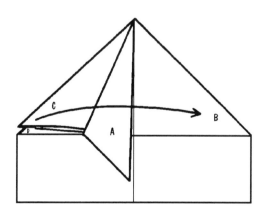

3. Fold flaps A and C to the right side.

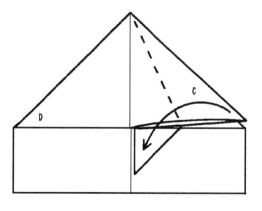

4. Fold flap C toward flap D, even with the center crease line.

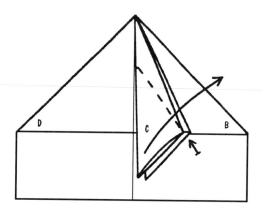

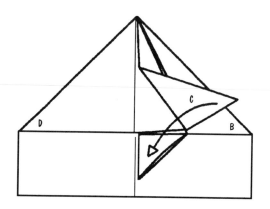

5. This is the wing folding step. Here you will learn two coordinate points to fold the wings out. First, you will need to know the pivot point (see small arrow). The coordinates here are 2 inches down from the tip, pivoting down to the edge angle as shown in this diagram. Fold the wing out to the right side.

6. Unfold.

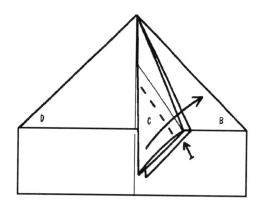

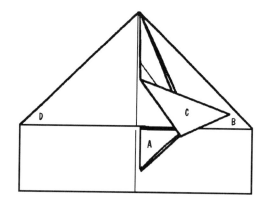

7. The second coordinates are 2¹/₂" from the tip, leaving ¹/₂" on the pivot point. Fold the wing to the right. You will see the difference between these two wing folds.

8. Wing fold completed.

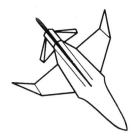

9. The Fuselage Fold

The fuselage fold is vital, the essential element needed to fold the planes in this book. Two coordinates will be given, as in the wing fold. Practice the fuselage fold a few times before starting on any plane. After this fold has been perfected, any fuselage can be folded with ease.

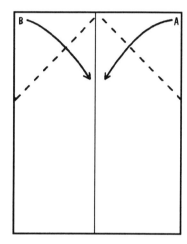

1. Begin with a center crease line. Fold corners A and B down to the center crease line.

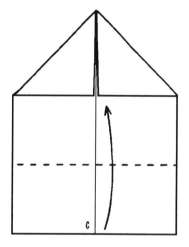

2. Fold C up to meet with the horizontal bottom edge of A and B.

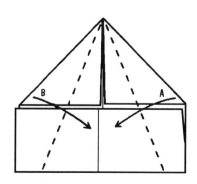

3. Fold A and B to the center line.

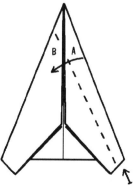

4. The coordinates for this fold are 2" down from the tip and $^1/2$" at the pivot point (indicated by the small arrow). Fold side A.

 Exquisite Interceptors

5. Unfold.

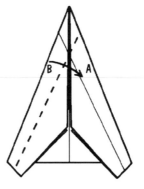

6. Fold side B.

7. Unfold.

8. This diagram shows the two resulting crease lines crossing.

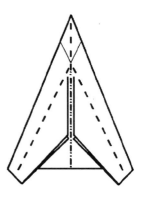

9. Make an inside reverse fold using the existing creases. The mountain crease rises up between the two outside edges. (Note: this is the fuselage reverse fold. The fuselage folds for the planes in this book have similar diagrams but different coordinates.)

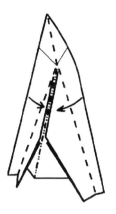

10. Proceed through the fold.

11. Flatten loosely.

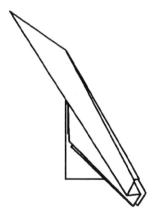

12. Fuselage fold completed.

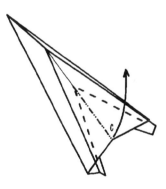

13. The tail fin of the plane. Here the inside reverse fold is going up.

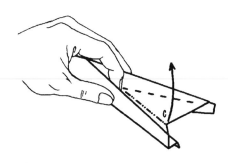

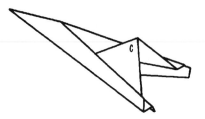

14. To make this reversal, hold the nose end of the plane with your left hand. Place your index finger in the center crease line as shown here. Hold the plane tightly at the nose end, control the size of the tail fin by sliding your index finger up or down the center crease line. At the lowest point of the belly, reverse it straight up the center with your right hand.

15. The inside reverse fold looks like this.

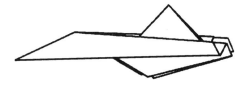

16. Completed tail fin fold.

Practice these last few important folds a few times until you are confident. Now you're ready to start folding real planes. You've earned your wings!

The Fleet

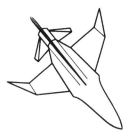

1. The Fly

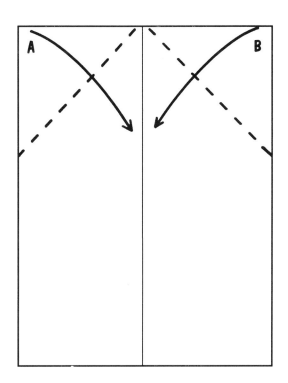

1. Fold A and B down to the center crease line.

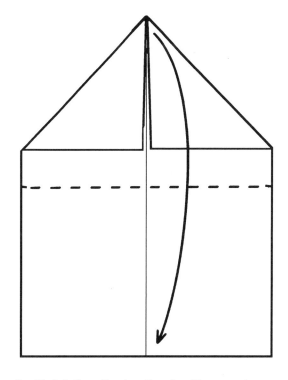

2. Fold the tip to the bottom edge.

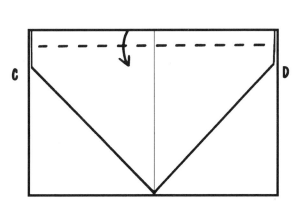

3. Fold top edge to line up with C and D.

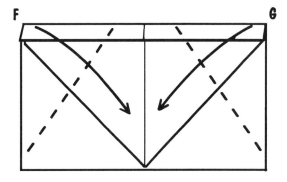

4. Fold F and G to the center, leaving approximately 1" from the center crease line on each side at the top edge, and $^{1}/_{2}$ " to the side edge at the two bottom corners. (An exact mea-surement is not vital here.)

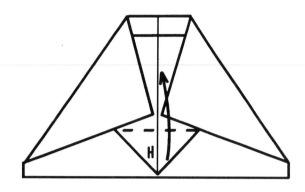

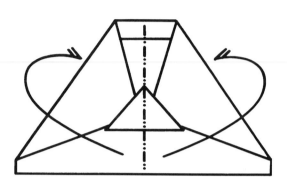

5. Fold H (the upside down triangle) up.

6. Mountain fold on the center crease line.

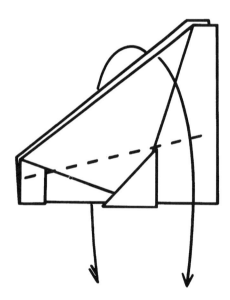

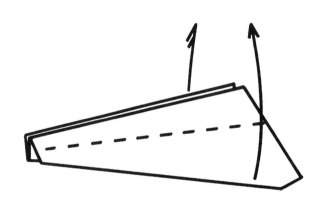

7. Fold the sides down, as shown here.

8. Fold the wings up.

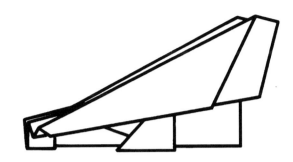

9. Wing folds complete.

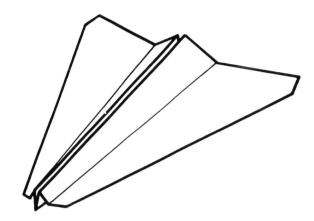

10. "The Fly" complete.

11. Front view.

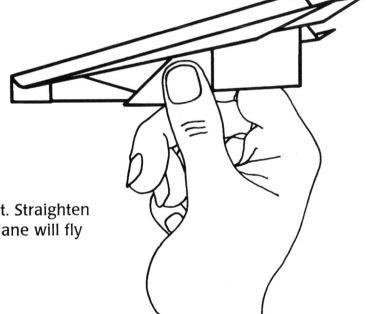

12. Holding position for flight. Straighten out the wings, and this plane will fly smoothly.

2. Solar Jet

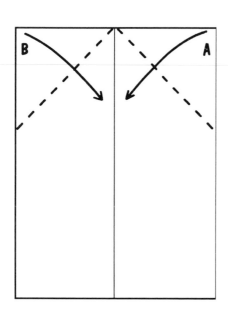

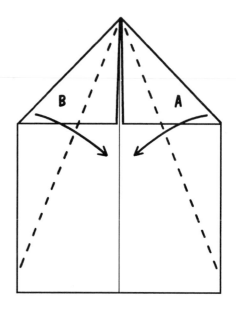

1. Fold A and B to the center crease line.

2. Fold A and B to the center crease line again.

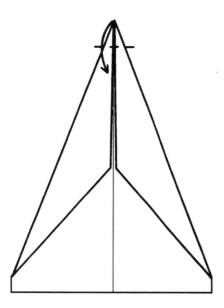

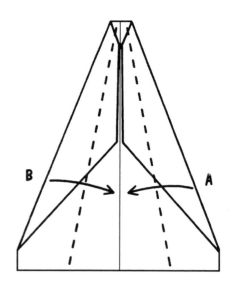

3. Fold down the tip approximately 1".

4. Fold A and B to the center crease line again.

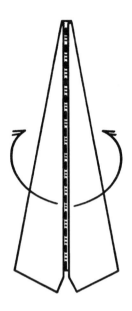

5. Mountain fold the plane in half.

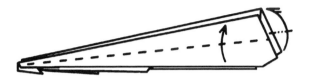

6. Fold both wings up to the top edge.

7. Wing fold completed.

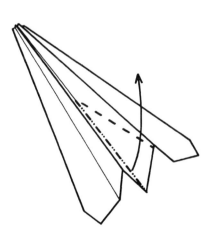

8. Reverse the tail fin.

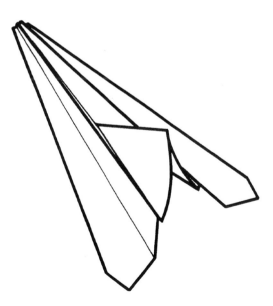

9. The tail fin fold looks like this.

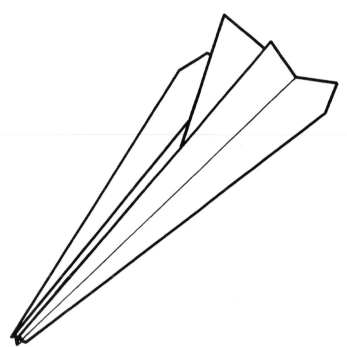

10. "Solar Jet" completed.

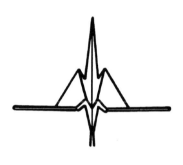

11. Front view.

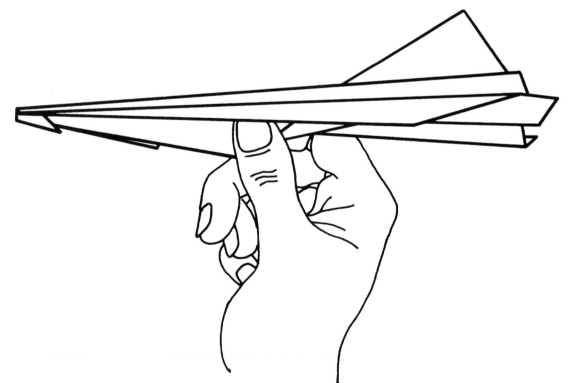

12. Holding position for flight. Throw the plane straight and it should fly smoothly.

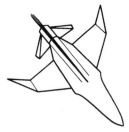

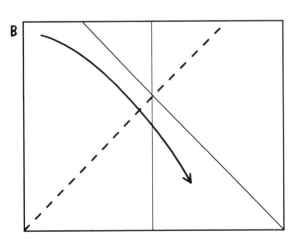

3. Bat Glider

Turn the paper sideways (horizontal), and make a center crease line.

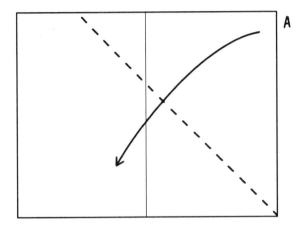

1. Fold A down diagonally toward the left side, align with bottom edge.

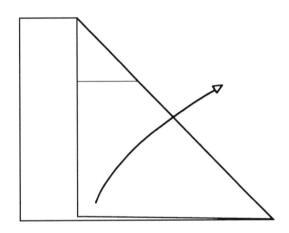

2. Unfold.

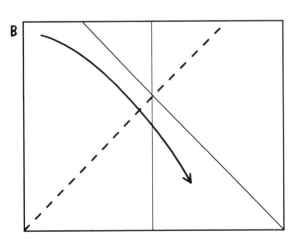

3. Fold B down diagonally toward the right side, align with bottom edge.

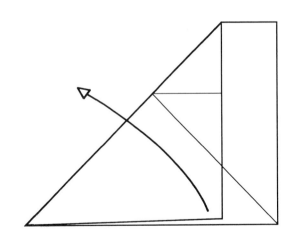

4. Unfold.

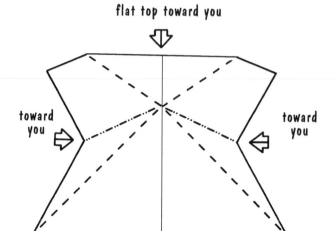

flat top toward you

toward you

toward you

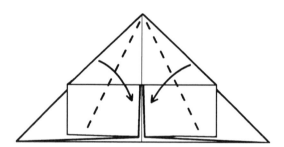

5. Make the waterbomb base.

6. The folding diagram for the waterbomb base. Note mountain and valley fold lines.

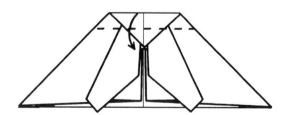

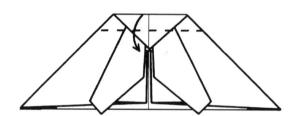

7. Waterbomb completed. Fold the two top flaps to the center line.

8. Fold the tip down to the center point.

9. Fold down again, to the center point.

10. Fold down again, along the edge of the last fold.

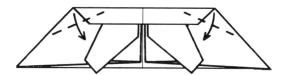

11. Fold down the two top corners.

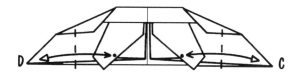

12. Fold C and D to the edge angle points as indicated by the dots, and unfold.

13. "Bat Glider" completed.

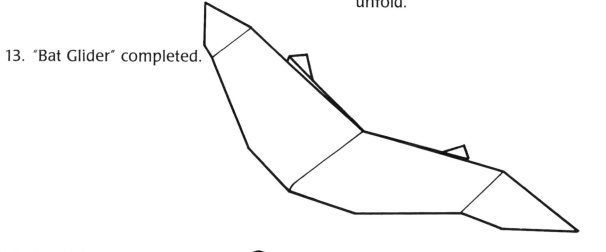

14. Front view.

15. Holding position for flight. Release this plane gently forward with a long follow-through and it will glide smoothly.

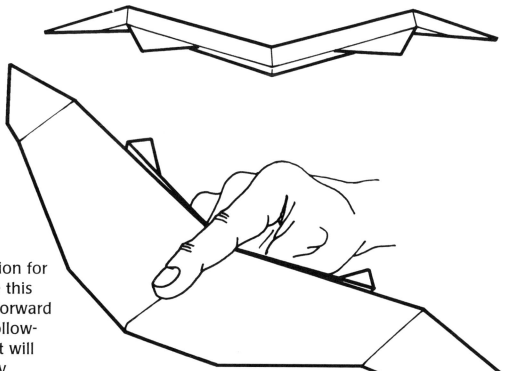

 Exquisite Interceptors

4. Manta Ray

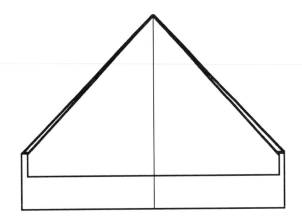

1. Begin with Base #2.

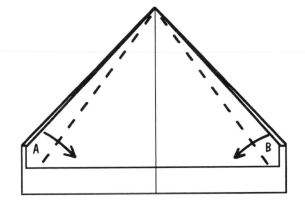

2. Fold A and B toward the center, with a pivot point of approximately ¼" (or a little bigger) to the corners of the top flaps.

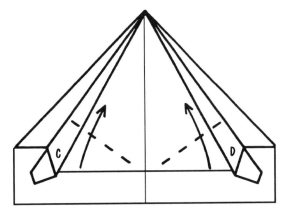

3. Fold C and D up so that the side edges line up with the upper half of the flap.

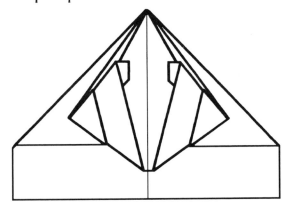

4. Turn the model over.

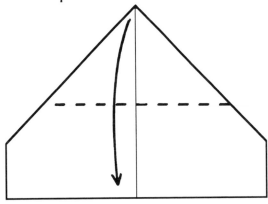

5. Fold the tip down to the bottom edge.

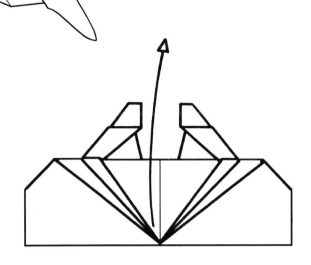

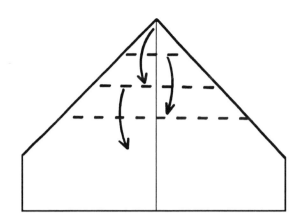

6. Unfold the previous fold.

7. Fold the tip halfway down to the horizontal crease (of the last fold), then fold again to the crease, and again on the crease.

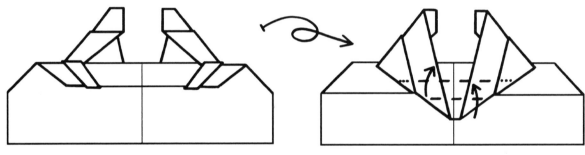

8. The finished fold looks like this. Turn the model over.

9. Fold the angled tip up halfway to the edge and then fold again to the edge.

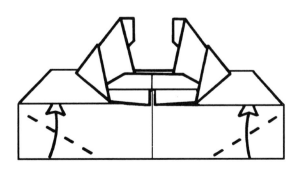

10. Fold the two bottom corners up under the above layer. The measurement should be approximately 2" from each side of the center line, leaving about ¼" on the side edge.

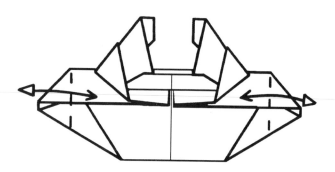

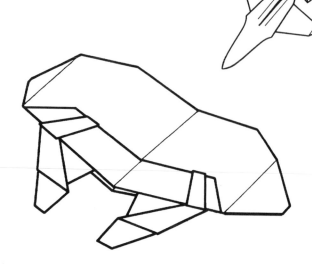

11. Fold both wing tips toward the center, then unfold.

12. Finished "Manta Ray."

13. Front view.

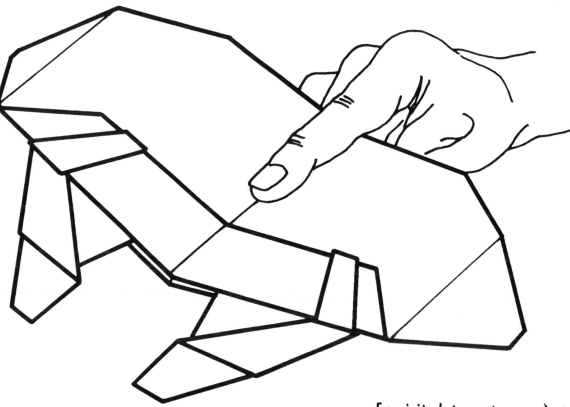

5. Prototype

The Prototype is simple to make and fly. It is designed mainly for practice. It will teach you control and help establish good folding techniques, which will build your confidence. This easy-to-make plane flies great indoors or out because of its large wingspan and well-balanced fuselage. Fold this plane a few times before moving on; the folds will be repeated in this order for all successive planes.

Begin with an unfinished Base #2. Don't unfold the base to make the waterbomb shape.

Your paper should look like this when you begin.

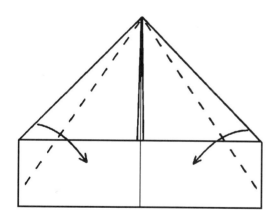

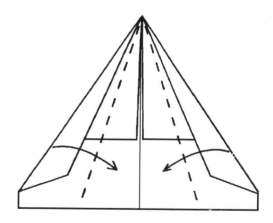

1. Fold the two sides toward the center, leaving ¾" to the side edges.

2. Fold both sides to the center crease line.

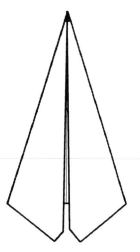

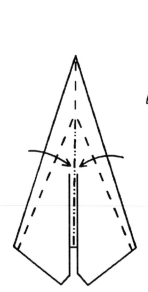

3. Your paper should now look like this.

4. Make the fuselage fold. Begin 2¾" down from the nose (or top) end, leaving ¼" to the two bottom corners. (Refer to the fuselage folding section if you're confused.)

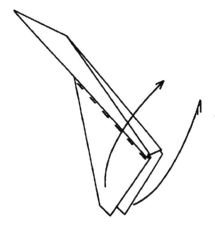

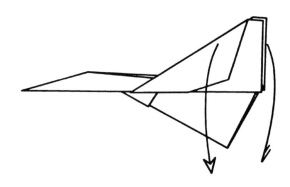

5. The fuselage fold should look like this. Fold both wings up.

6. Unfold the wings.

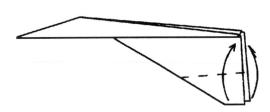

7. Fold both wing tips up by half.

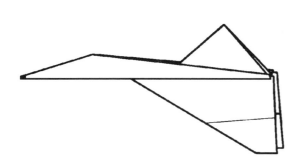

8. Unfold the tips.

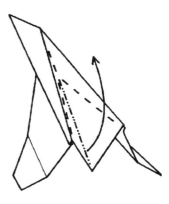

9. Make an inside reverse fold for the tail fin. (Refer to the inside reverse fold section on page 12 if you don't remember how to do this.)

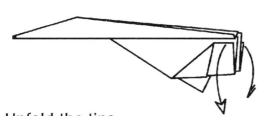

10. The tail fin fold should look like this.

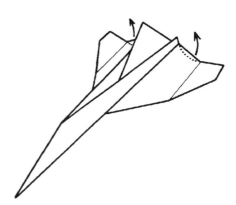

11. Adjust the wings to make sure they are even, and bend the elevators up to provide lift.

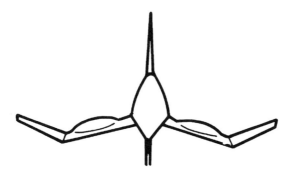

12. Front view (elevators up).

 Exquisite Interceptors

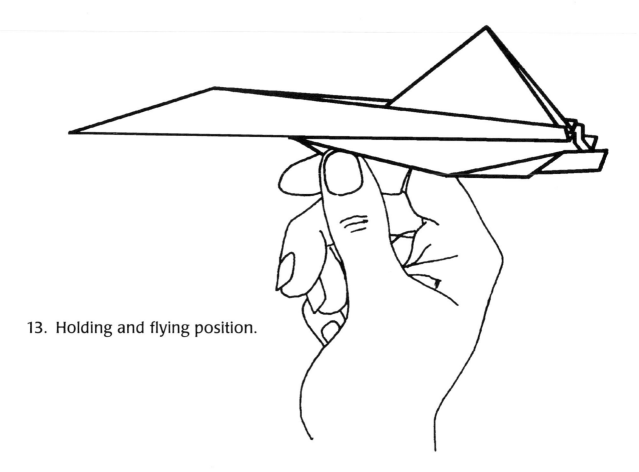

13. Holding and flying position.

Check to make sure the wings are even, then throw it! It should soar like a real jet, but if the plane pitches up or down, adjust it by raising or lowering the elevators. If the plane darts to one side, an elevator may be bent too far or not bent far enough. Trim the elevators a little for better overall control of the plane.

6. Lightning Jet

Turn the paper sideways (horizontal), and make a center crease line.

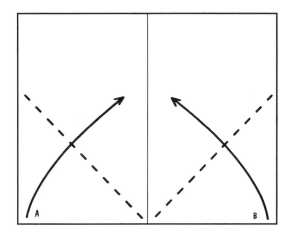

1. Fold up A and B to the center crease line.

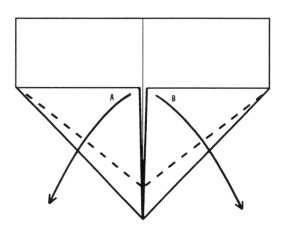

2. Fold A and B down approxi-mately 1¼" from the upside-down tip, as shown.

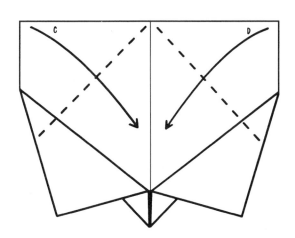

3. Fold C and D to the Center crease line.

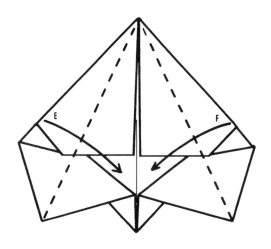

4. Fold E and F to the center crease line on the tip and the two bottom corners.

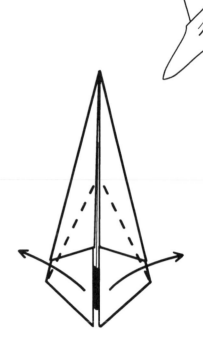

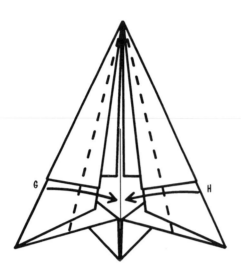

5. Fold G and H to the center.

6. Approximately 3½" from the tip, fold the wings out pivoting from the center.

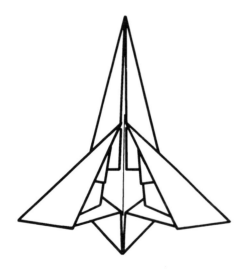

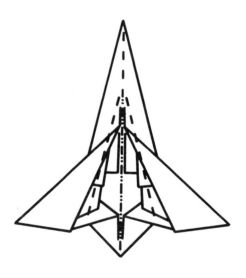

7. Your paper should look like this.

8. Approximately 2½" from the tip and ½" at the pivot point, make the fuselage reverse fold.

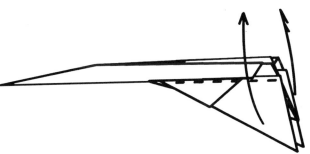

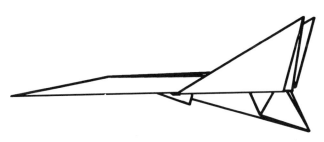

9. The completed fuselage fold. Fold wings up along the edge line on both sides.

10. The completed wing fold.

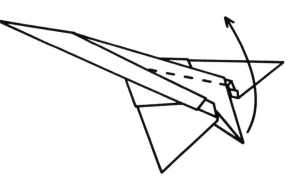

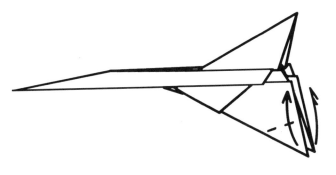

11. Reverse the tail fin up about 1½" high.

12. Fold the end points of the wings up.

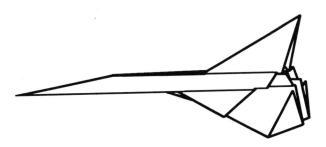

13. The end point folds look like this.

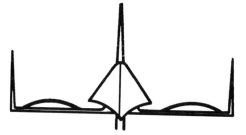

14. Completed "Lightning Jet." For lift, bend up the trailing edge of the wings slightly.

15. Front view.

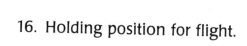

16. Holding position for flight.

7. Fire Fox

Begin with Base #2.

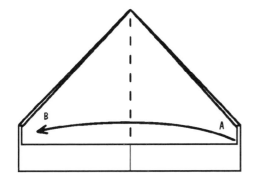

1. Flip A to the left side.

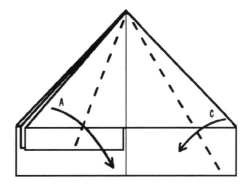

2. Fold A to the center line, then fold C toward the center with ½" between the valley fold line and the bottom right corner.

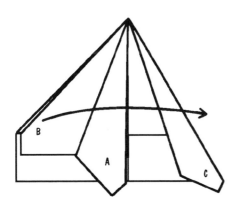

3. Flip A and B to the right side.

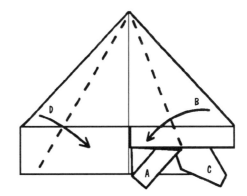

4. Fold B and D to match A and C.

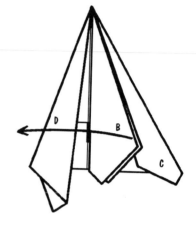

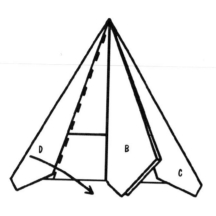

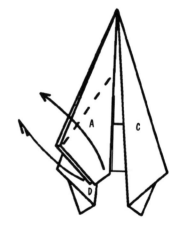

5. Fold D toward the center along the edge of the prior fold.

6. Flip B and A to the left side.

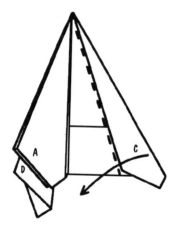

7. Fold C toward the center along the edge of the prior fold.

8. Approximately 2½" from the tip, fold both wings (A and B) out, pivoting from the center.

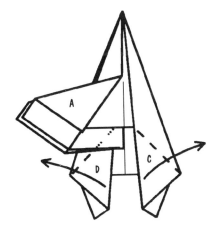

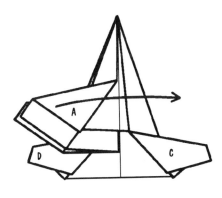

9. Fold both tail fins (C and D) out to the side between the middle edge and the two lower corners.

10. Flip wing flap A to the right side.

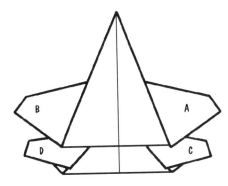

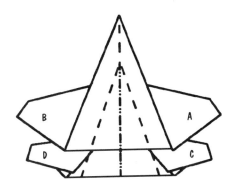

11. Your paper should look like this.

12. Make the fuselage reverse fold, 1¾" from the tip and ½" at the pivot point.

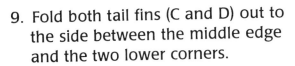

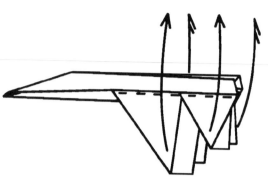

13. Fold the wings and stabilizers up along the edge of the fuselage.

14. Fold both of the wings in half (downward) and make a reverse fold for the belly.

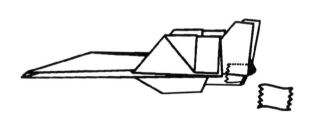

15. Tape the edges under the tail fins.

16. Bend up the trailing edge of the wings for lift, and the plane is finished.

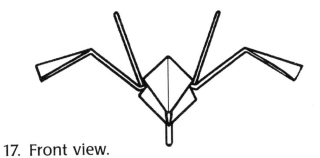

17. Front view.

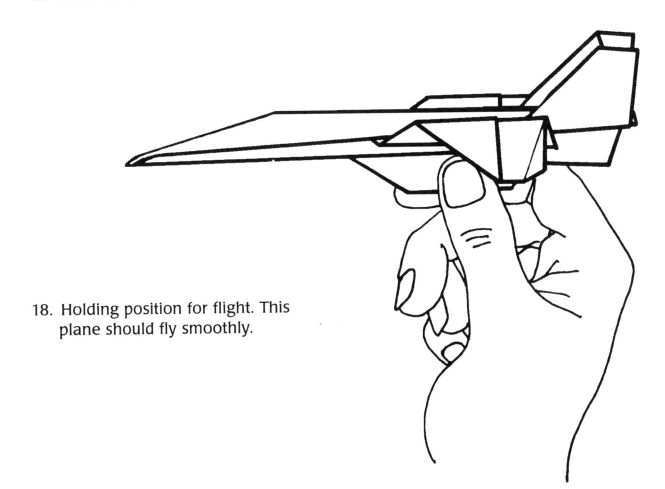

18. Holding position for flight. This plane should fly smoothly.

8. Wind Jet

Turn the paper sideways (horizontally), and make a center crease line.

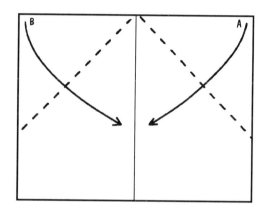

1. Fold A and B to the center line.

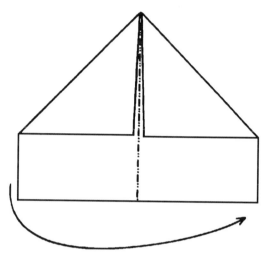

2. Mountain fold B to the right side.

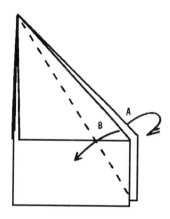

3. Fold A and B toward the center, leaving ½" of the outside edge.

   (A will fold left, and B will fold right. This is a matching fold.)

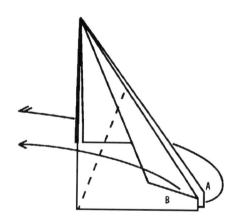

4. Approximately 3½" from the tip on the slope side, angled down to the center crease line, fold B leftward and A rightward.

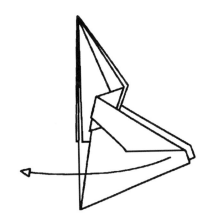

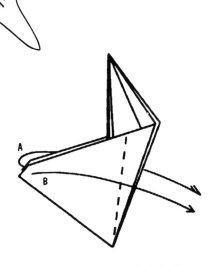

5. Fold B rightward and A leftward on line between the fuselage edges.

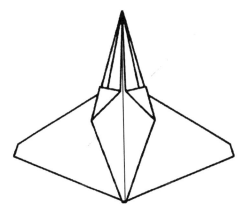

6. Fold model open flat.

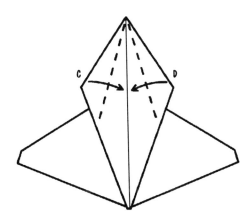

7. Fold C and D to the center crease line.

8. Your paper should look like this.

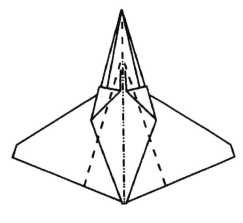

9. Approximately 2" from the tip and 1½" from the bottom point to the end of the fold line, make the fuselage fold.

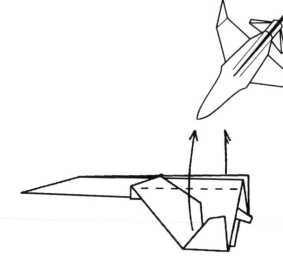

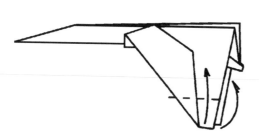

10. Fold each wing tip up about 1".

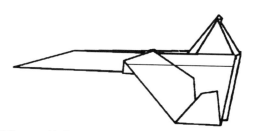

11. Fold the wings up. Note fold line.

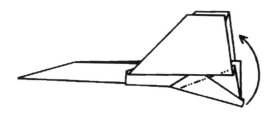

12. Reverse the tail fin up, then bring the wings back down.

13. The tail fin should look like this.

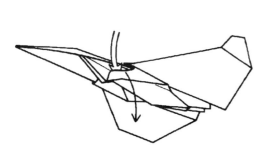

14. Dig out the intakes. (This is an optional fold.)

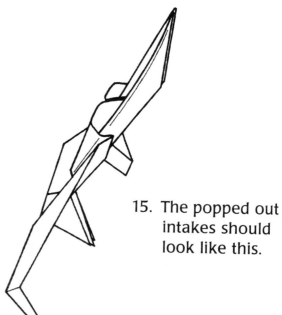

15. The popped out intakes should look like this.

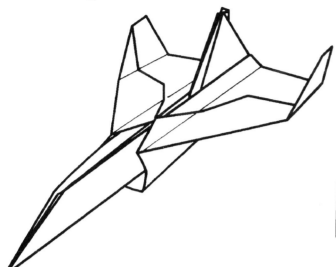

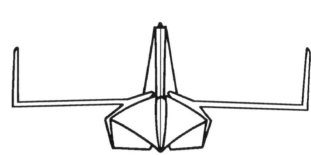

16. Completed "Wind Jet."

17. Front view.

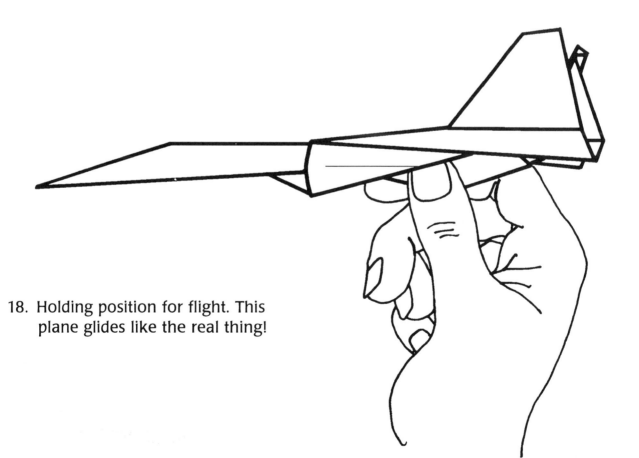

18. Holding position for flight. This plane glides like the real thing!

9. Crow

Turn the paper horizontally, and make a center crease line.

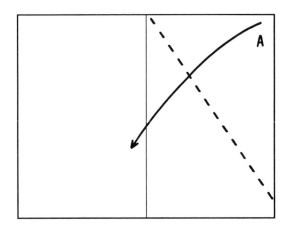

1. Fold A diagonally down to the left side at the top end (tip) of the crease line leaving ¾" for the side edge.

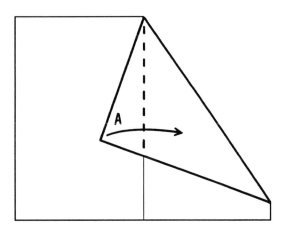

2. Fold A to the right side as shown, using the center crease line as a guide.

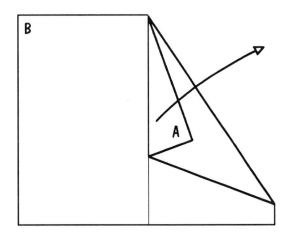

3. Unfold.

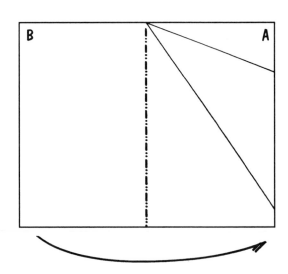

4. Fold B behind to the right side.

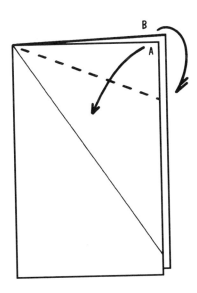
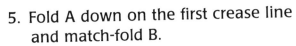

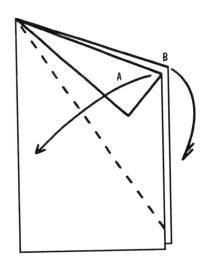

5. Fold A down on the first crease line and match-fold B.

6. Fold A down on the second crease line and match-fold B.

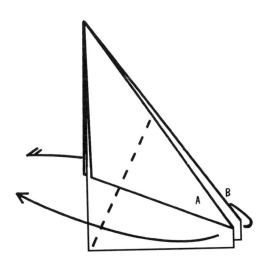

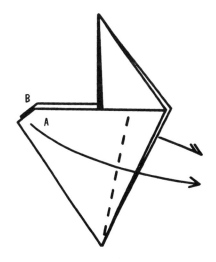

7. Approximately 4½" from the tip to the top end of the fold line, fold A to the left side, pivoting from corner of the center crease line. Match-fold B.

8. Fold A to the right between the right angle and the vertical edge. Match-fold B.

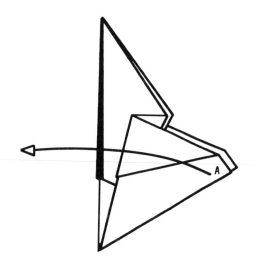

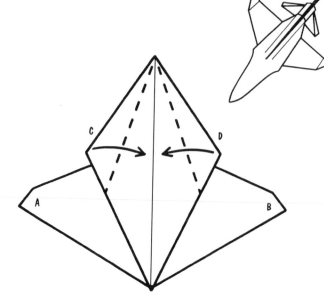

9. Flip model open flat.

10. Fold C and D to the center line.

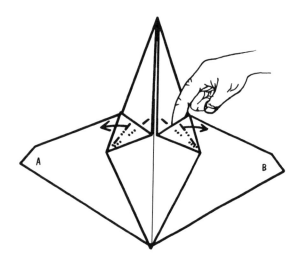

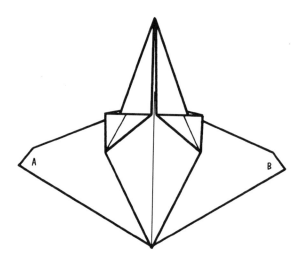

11. Dig out the pockets and squash them flat.

12. Turn the model over.

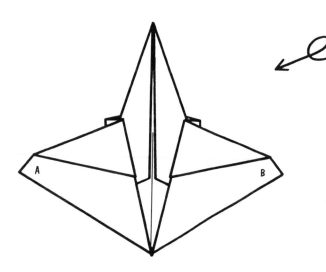

13. Your paper should look like this.

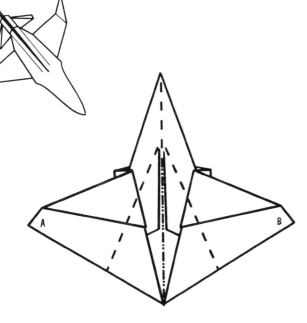

14. Make the fuselage fold about 2½" down from the tip and 2¼" from the bottom angle point to the fold lines on each side.

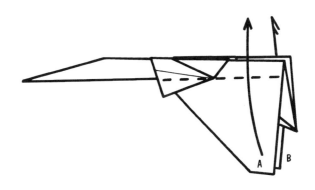

15. Fold both wings (A and B) up.

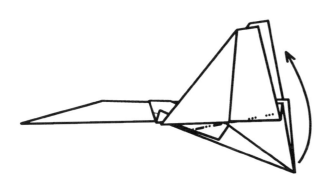

16. Make an inside reverse fold for the tail fin, and bring the wings down.

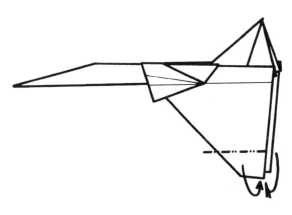

17. Mountain fold both wings ¾" to the inside (toward the belly of the plane).

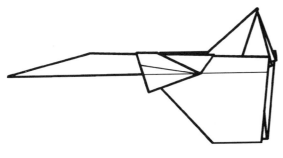

18. The fold should look like this.

Exquisite Interceptors

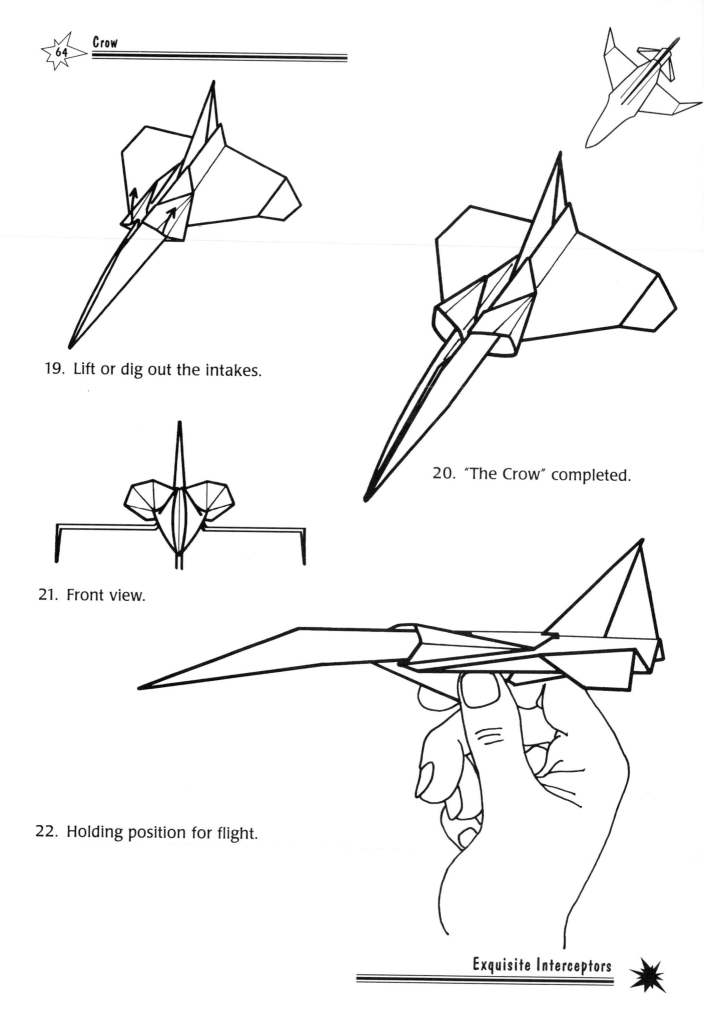

19. Lift or dig out the intakes.

20. "The Crow" completed.

21. Front view.

22. Holding position for flight.

10. Cobra

Begin with Base #1.

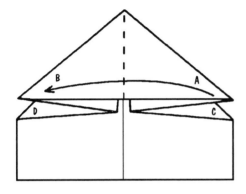

1. Flip A to the left side.

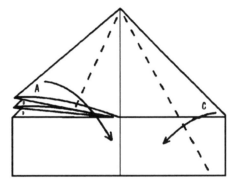

2. Fold A to the center crease line, and C toward the center crease line with approximately ½" between the bottom corner and the fold line.

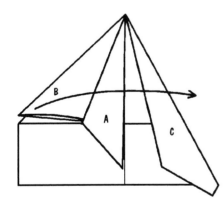

3. Flip A and B to the left side.

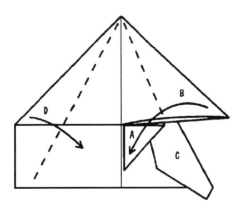

4. Fold B and D toward the center line to match the other side.

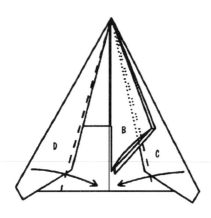

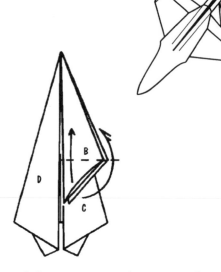

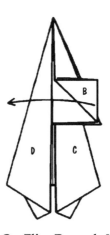

5. Fold C and D to the center crease line.

6. Fold B and A up, op-posite to each other.

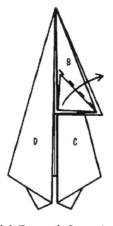

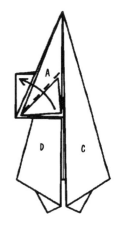

7. Fold B and A out along the slanted edge.

8. Flip B and A to the left.

9. Match fold this side to the other side.

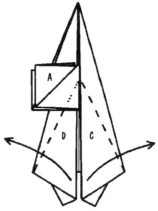

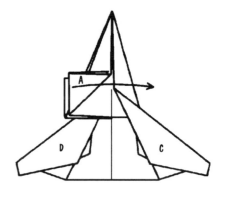

10. About 3" from the tip, fold the wings (D and C) out to the side, pivoting from the center crease line angle.

11. Flip A to the right side.

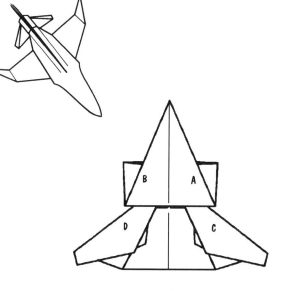

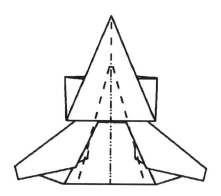

12. Your paper should look like this.

13. Make the fuselage fold about 1½"
from the tip and ½" at the pivot
point.

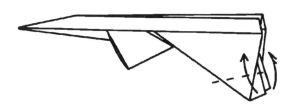

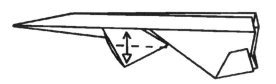

14. Fold up the wing end at a slant (do
this for both sides).

15. Fold the intake up to the edge of the
fuselage and back (do this for both
sides).

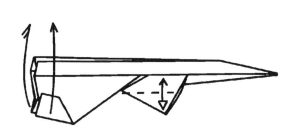

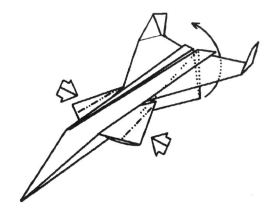

16. Lift the wings up.

17. Push in or pop the side of the plane
to create the intakes and reverse
the tail fin, folding it up.

18. Fold the wings up along the edge of the fuselage, then unfold.

19. Fold the two excess layers under the nose inward to make a narrow nose for the plane.

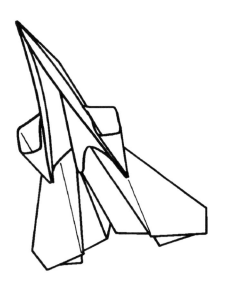

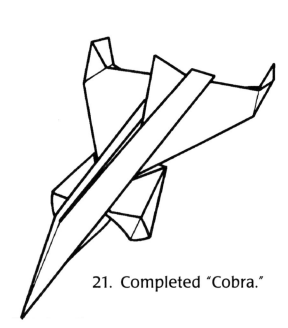

20. The excess layer fold looks like this.

21. Completed "Cobra."

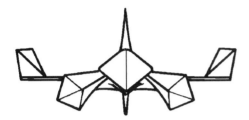

22. Front view.

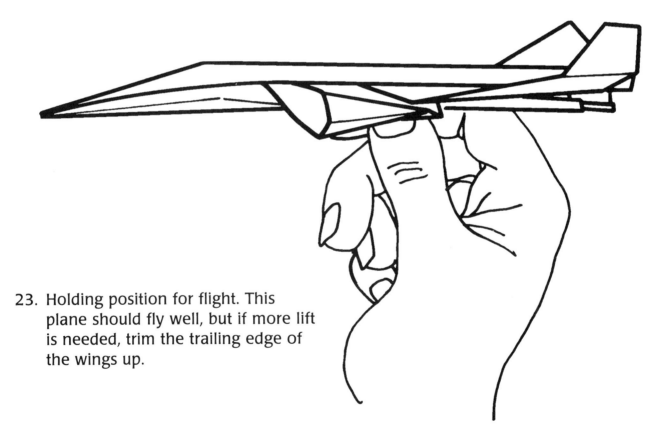

23. Holding position for flight. This plane should fly well, but if more lift is needed, trim the trailing edge of the wings up.

11. Delta-X

Begin with Base #1.

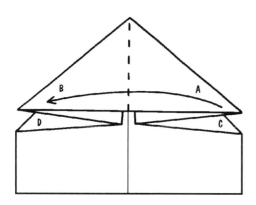

1. Flip A to the left side.

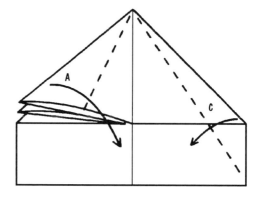

2. Fold A to the center, and C toward the center, leaving ½" of the outside edge.

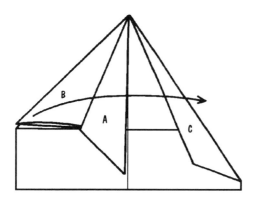

3. Flip A and B to the right side.

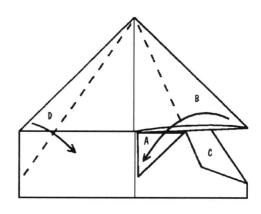

4. Fold B and D toward the center to match the other side.

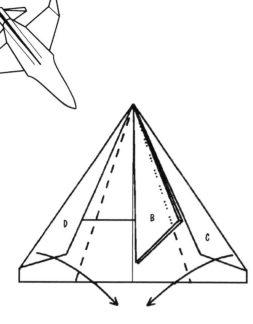

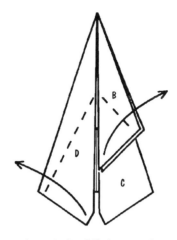

5. Fold C and D to the center line.

6. Approximately 3" from the tip, and on pivot points ¼" from ouside edges, fold out B and D as shown.

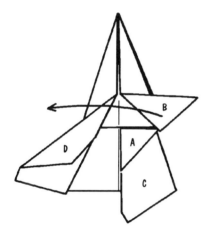

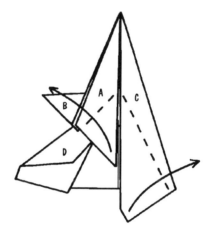

7. Flip B and A to the left side.

8. Fold A and C to match the other side.

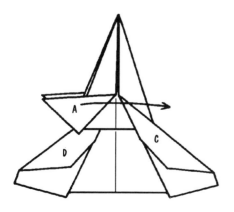

9. Flip A to the right side.

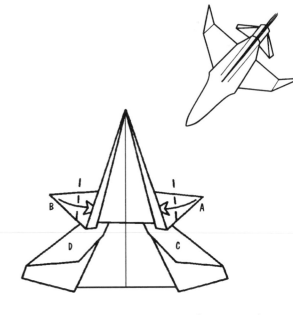

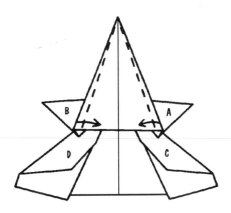

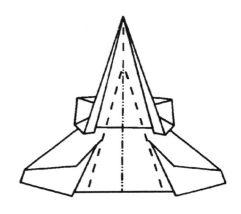

10. Make a narrow fold along A and B toward the middle, from the tip and the two small angles.

11. Fold under the two points (A and B) as shown.

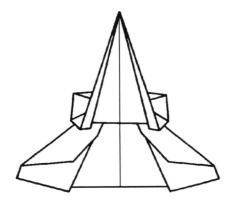

12. Your paper should look like this.

13. Approximately 2" from the tip and on pivot points ½" from inside paper edges (as shown), fold the fuselage.

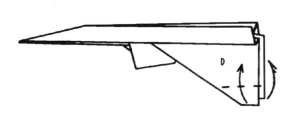

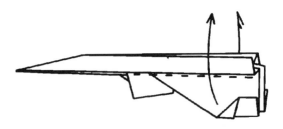

14. Fold both wings up ½".

15. Fold both wings up along the edge of the fuselage.

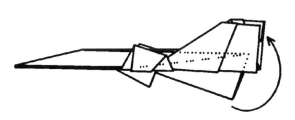

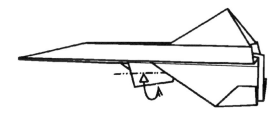

16. Reverse the tail fin up.

17. Mountain fold half of the intake to the back, then turn the model over.

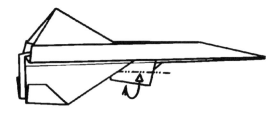

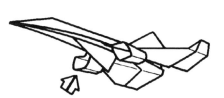

18. Mountain fold this intake in half.

19. Pop the intakes to look like this.

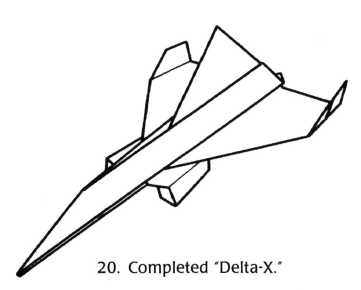

20. Completed "Delta-X."

21. Front view.

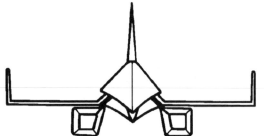

22. Holding position for flight.

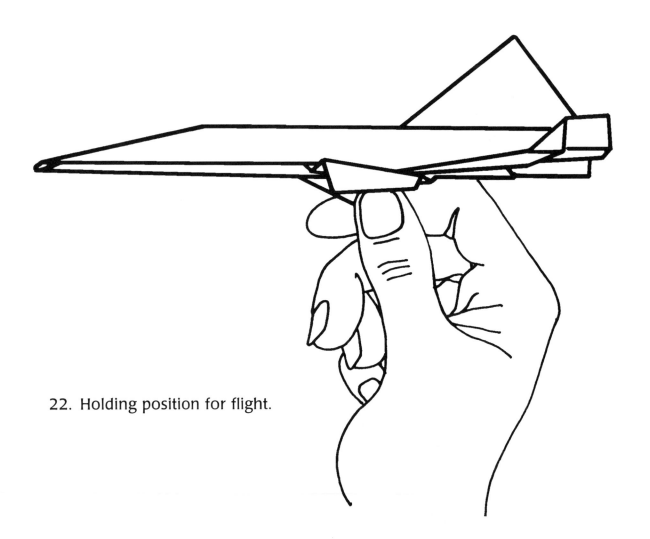

12. Fire Bird

Turn the paper horizontally, and make a center crease line.

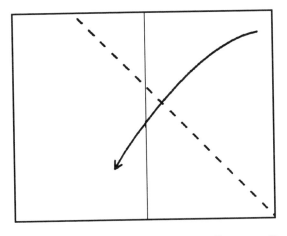

1. Fold the top right corner diagonally down to the left bottom edge.

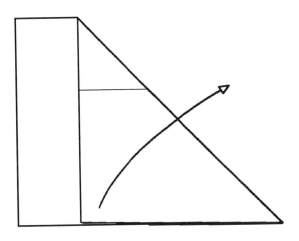

2. Unfold.

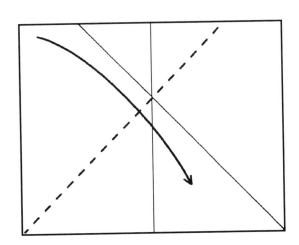

3. Fold the left corner diagonally down to the right bottom edge.

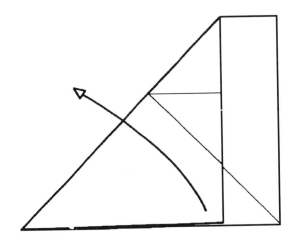

4. Unfold.

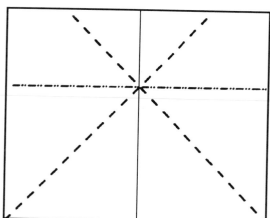

5. Ready.

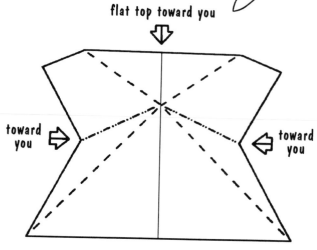

flat top toward you

toward you

toward you

6. Make the familiar waterbomb base.

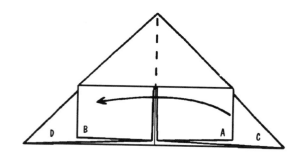

7. Waterbomb completed. Flip A to the left side.

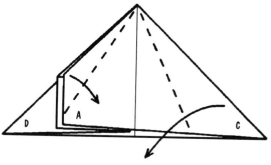

8. Fold A toward the center crease line, leaving approximately 1/2" to the outside edge, and fold C to the center crease line.

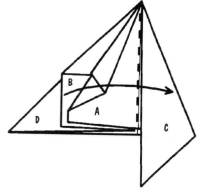

9. Flip A and B to the right side.

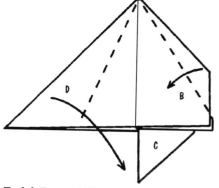

10. Fold B and C toward the center to match the other side.

Exquisite Interceptors

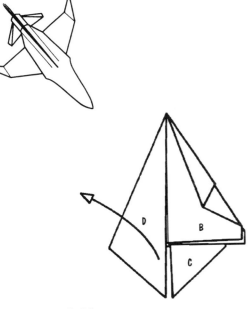

11. Unfold.

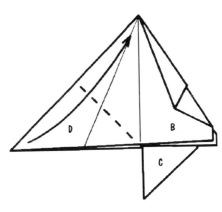

12. Fold the corner of D up to the tip.

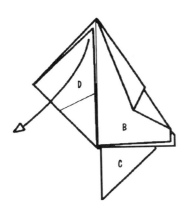

13. Unfold.

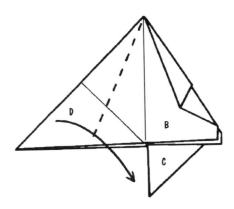

14. Fold D to the center on the crease line.

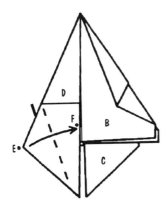

15. Fold dot E to dot F, as shown, leaving a little of the bottom edge.

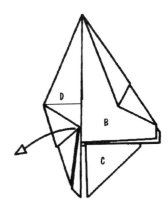

16. Unfold side completely.

Exquisite Interceptors

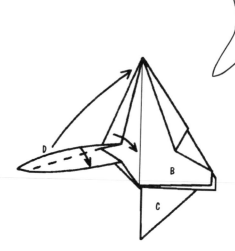

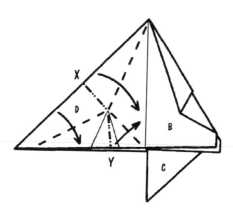

17. Pinch points X and Y toward you. (Note mountain and valley folds.)

18. Fold D up to tip.

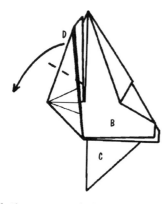

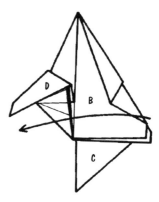

19. Fold the wing (D) down diagonally so that the right edge of the wing overlaps the top crease line.

20. Flip B and A to the left side.

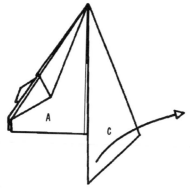

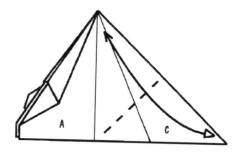

21. Unfold C to the right.

22. Fold C up diagonally to the tip, then unfold.

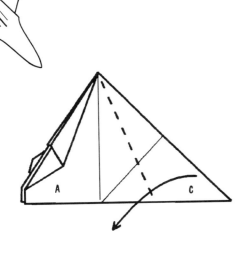

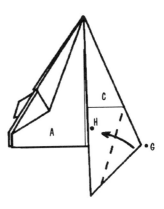

23. Fold C to the center again on the crease line.

24. Fold dot G to dot H, as shown.

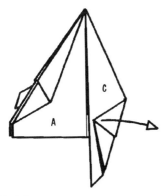

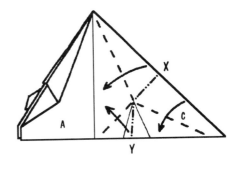

25. Unfold.

26. Look back at step 17 and copy action for this side.

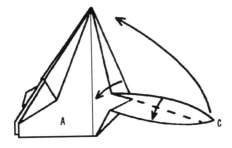

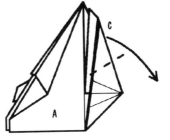

27. Fold C as shown by the arrows.

28. Fold the wing (C) to the right. The left edge of the wing should overlap the top crease line.

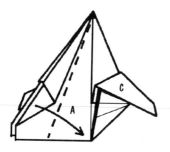

29. Fold A to the center (toward C).

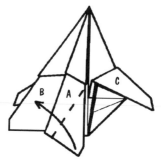

30. Approximately 3½" from the tip and on pivot point as shown, fold the stabilizer to the left side, as shown.

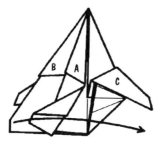

31. Flip A and B to the right side.

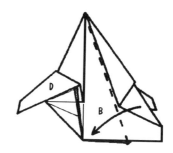

32. Fold B to the center.

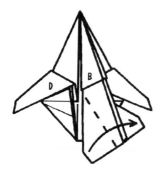

33. Match fold B like A.

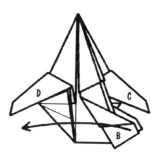

34. Flip stabilizer B to left.

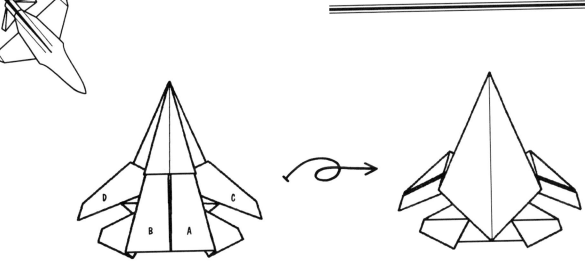

35. Turn the model over.

36. Your paper should look like this.

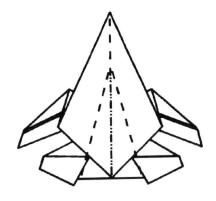

37. Approximately 1¾" down from the tip and the bottom angle edge, make the fuselage fold.

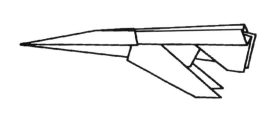

38. The fold looks like this.

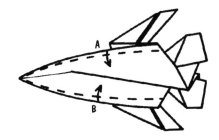

39. Fold edges of A and B toward the center to look like this. This fold narrows the nose.

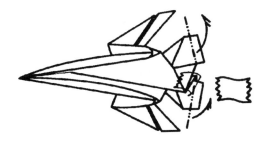

40. Tape as shown and bend the stabilizers up.

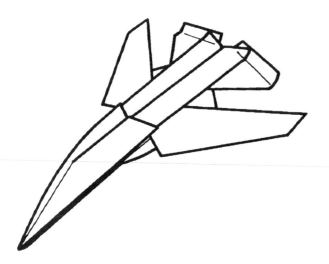

41. Completed "Fire Bird."

42. Front view.

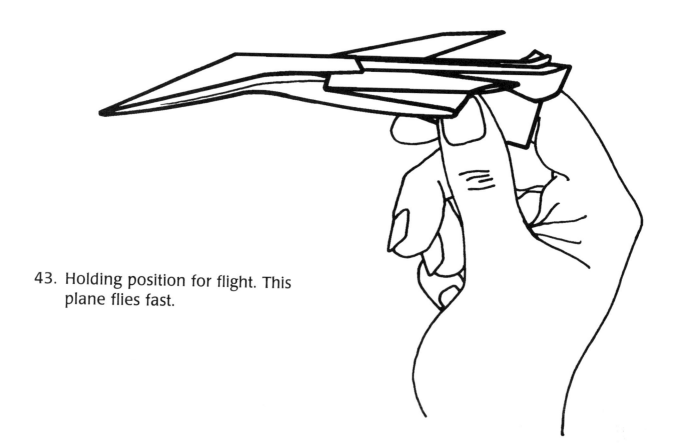

43. Holding position for flight. This plane flies fast.

13. Aerial Bird

You can use Base Fold (2) on this plane and skip to step 7, but for fun try this new method:

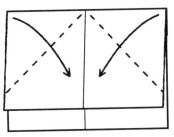

2. Fold the top two corners to the center crease line.

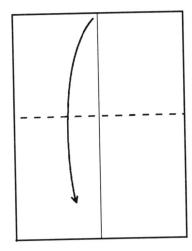

1. Fold the paper down 4¾" as shown.

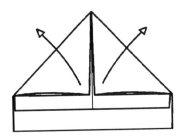

3. Unfold the paper as shown.

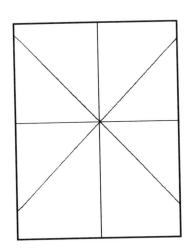

4. The paper should have these creases. Turn the model over.

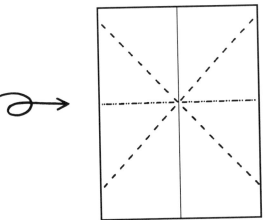

5. Press the center point with your finger, to shape the waterbomb.

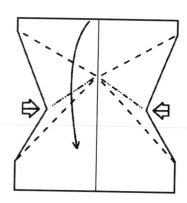

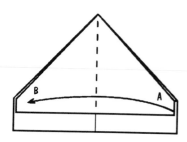

6. The folding diagram for the familiar waterbomb base.

7. The completed base. Fold A to the left side.

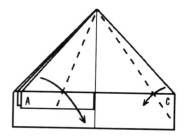

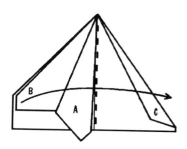

8. Fold A to the center and C toward the center, leaving approximately ¼" on the outside edge.

9. Fold A and B to the right side.

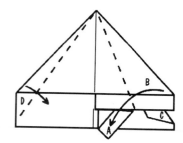

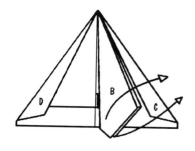

10. Match fold B and D (like A and C).

11. Unfold A and B.

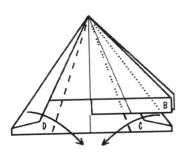

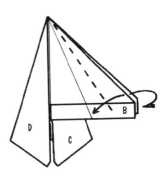

12. Fold D and C to the center crease line.

13. Fold A and B to the crease line in opposite directions.

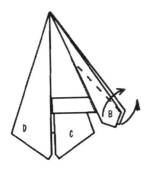

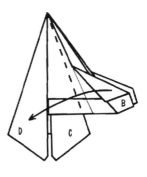

14. Approximately 3" from the tip, fold out A and B at an angle, as shown.

15. Fold B to the center.

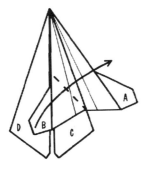

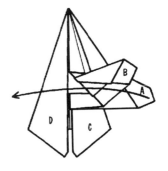

16. Approximately 3" from the tip, fold the wing (B) out.

17. Fold A and B to the left side.

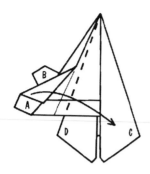

18. Fold A to the center.

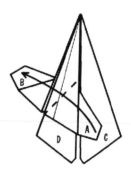

19. Match fold wing A like wing B.

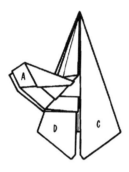

20. Turn the model over.

21. Fold corners of C and D to the center.

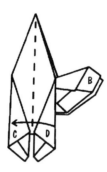

22. Flip D to the left.

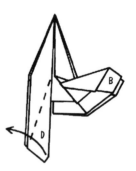

23. Approximately 3" from the tip, fold the tail out.

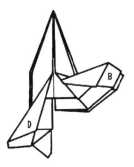  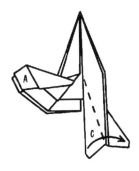

24. Turn the model over.

25. Repeat steps 21, 22, 23 for flap C.

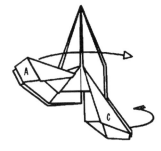

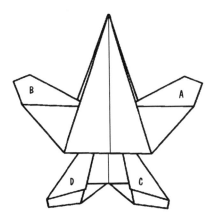

26. Flip A to the right and D to the left.

27. Your paper should now look like this.

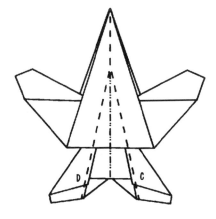

28. Make the fuselage fold approximately 1¾" down from the tip to the two inside angles (of C and D) at the bottom edge.

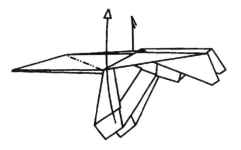

29. Unfold both sides to look like this.

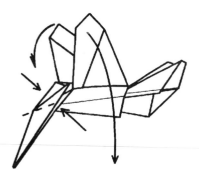

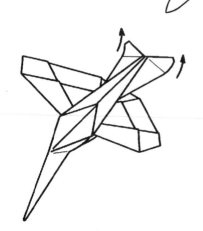

30. Fold the sides down to their previous positions, and a new fold will occur at the valley fold line. Pinch tightly where the two small arrows are pointing. Stretch the nose forward to balance the bird in flight.

31. Bend the tail up, and this bird is ready to fly.

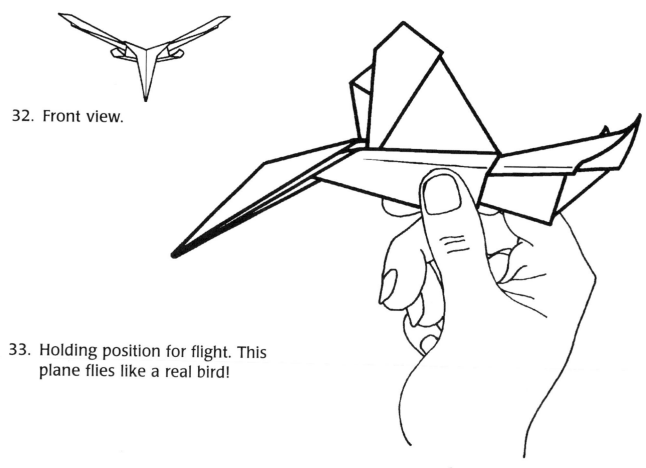

32. Front view.

33. Holding position for flight. This plane flies like a real bird!

14. Saab Draken

The Saab Draken was built in the '50s, and was still in service in the '90s. Built by the Saab company to defend Sweden's territories, the Draken's design boasts a double delta wing configuration that sweeps back at an angle of 80° for the forward portion and 57° for the rear main wing section. This plane can take off from a roadside airstrip, intercept an enemy plane flying at Mach 2, then land again on a chosen roadside. Fitted with Europe's most powerful radar, the Saab Draken is a sophisticated and agile fighter that will remain on the cutting edge of Sweden's technology well into the future.

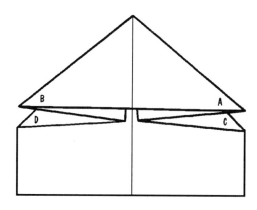

1. Begin with Base Fold 1.

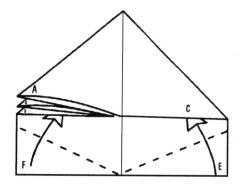

2. Flip A to the left side, fold E and F up and under C and D, leaving approximately ½" to the outside edge.

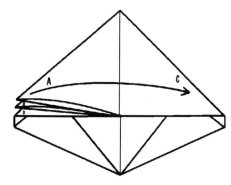

3. Flip A and B to the right side.

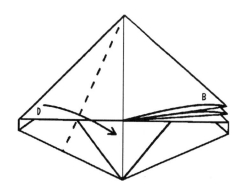

4. Fold D to the center crease line.

Exquisite Interceptors

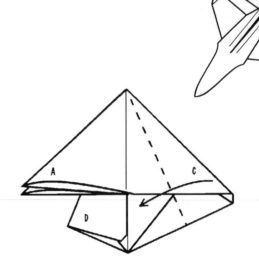

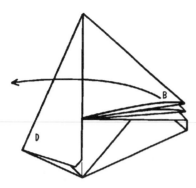

5. Flip B and A to the left side.

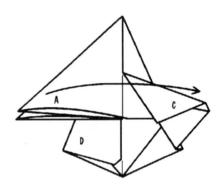

6. Fold C to the center crease line.

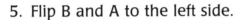

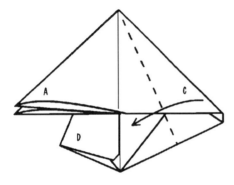

7. Approximately 2½" from the tip and ¼" at the pivot point, fold the wing (C) out.

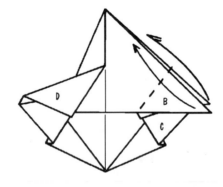

8. Flip A and B to the right side.

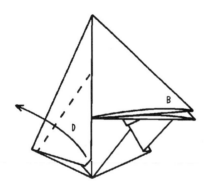

9. Repeat step 7 for flap D.

10. On the slope side of the wings (A and B), fold ⅓ of the wing up diagonally.

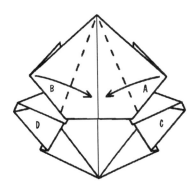

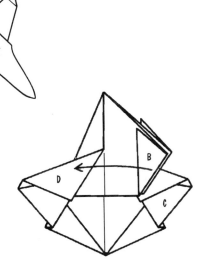

11. Flip B to the left side.

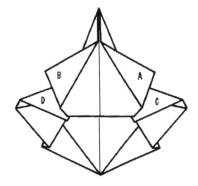

12. Fold A and B to the center crease line.

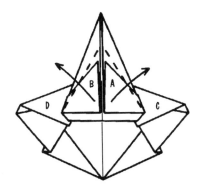

13. Approximately 1½" down from the tip, fold out A and B at an angle, as shown.

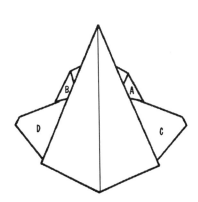

14. Turn the model over.

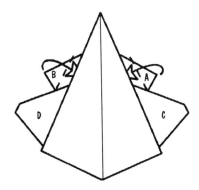

15. Fold A and B under the edges of the fuselage.

16. Turn the model over.

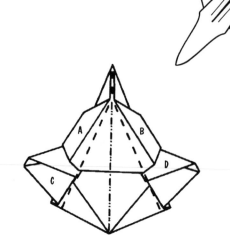

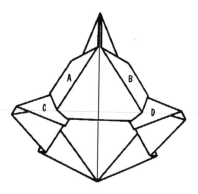

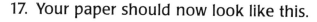

17. Your paper should now look like this.

18. Approximately 1½" inches down from the tip, with a pivot point of ½" on both sides, make the fuselage fold.

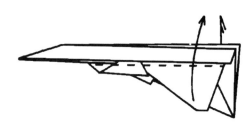

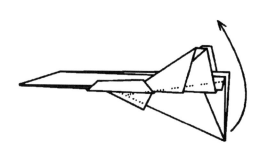

19. Fold both wings up.

20. Reverse the tail fin up.

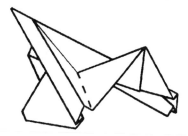

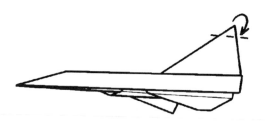

21. The reversed tail fin should look like this.

22. Reverse the tip of the tail fin down about ½".

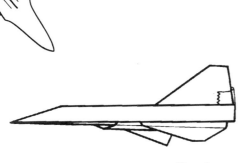

23. Tape as shown, or tape the two edges under the tail fin.

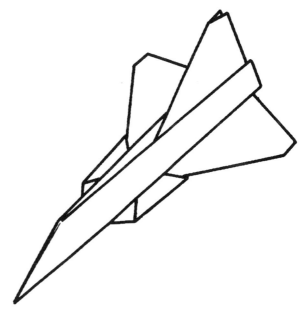

24. Completed "Saab Draken."

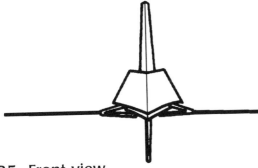

25. Front view.

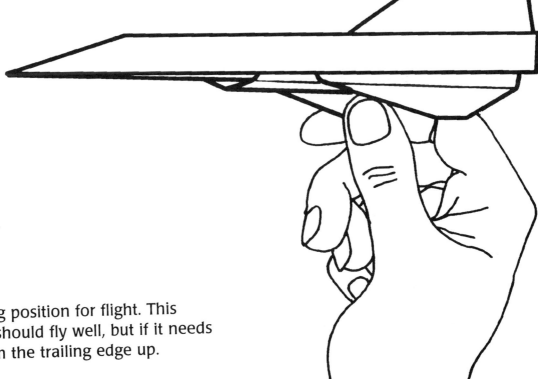

26. Holding position for flight. This plane should fly well, but if it needs lift, trim the trailing edge up.

15. YF-23

United States planes like the F-15 Eagle were once top tactical fighters, but as Soviet planes like the Mig-27 and SU-7 Flanker began surpassing it in maneuverability and performance, the US sought to develop a more advanced tactical fighter and to maintain its edge in technology and design. The YF-23 has a unique shape, with large triangular wings and tail fins that sweep back at a 45° angle. The maiden flight of the YF-23 took place on August 27, 1990 at 7:15 am.

This sophisticated plane remains an experimental model, a prototype for future fighter planes.

Begin with Base Fold 2.

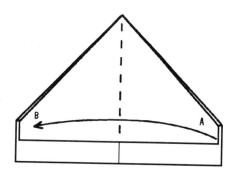

1. Flip A to the left side.

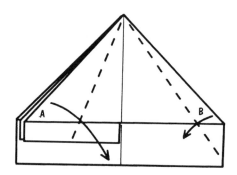

2. Fold A to the center crease line and C toward the center leaving approximately ¼" to the side edge at the bottom.

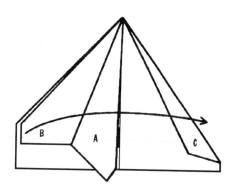

3. Flip A and B to the right.

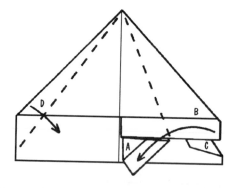

4. Repeat steps 2 and 3 for flap D.

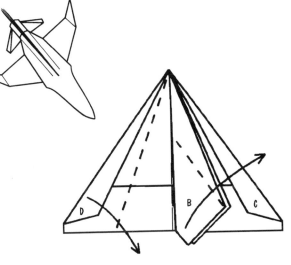

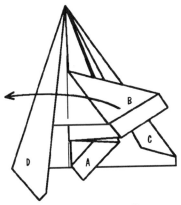

5. Fold D to the center approximately 1¾" from the bottom left corner to the fold line and fold the wing (B) out about 2¼" from the tip pivoting from the center crease line.

6. Both folds look like this. Flip A and B to the left side.

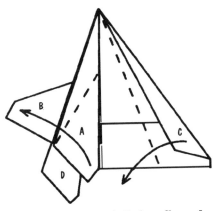

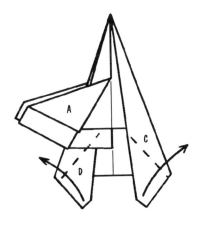

7. Repeat steps 5 and 6 for flap A and C (to match folds for B and D).

8. Approximately 2½" up from the bottom angles of C and D, fold the stabilizer out, with a ¼" pivot point.

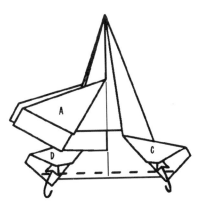

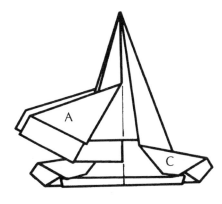

9. Fold the bottom edge just enough to fit under C and D.

10. The finished fold should look like this.

 Exquisite Interceptors

Focus on the wings:

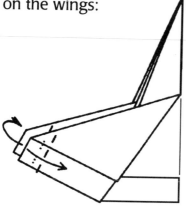

11. Fold (in opposite directions) ½" of both wings toward the center.

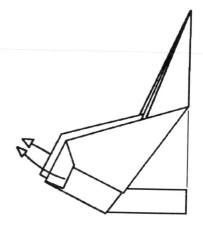

12. Unfold.

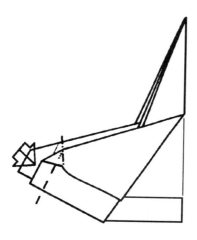

13. Make an inside reverse fold as shown.

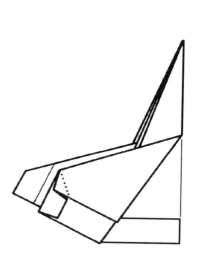

14. The completed inside reverse fold. Turn the model over.

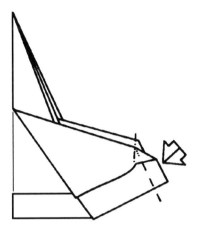

15. Make an inside reverse fold on wing tip.

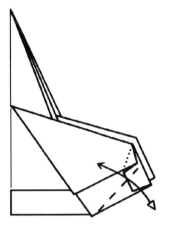

16. Fold wing tip as shown, then unfold.

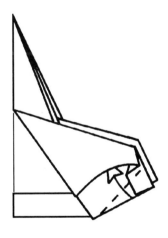

17. Refold under the top layer.

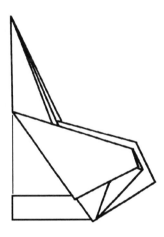

18. Wing fold complete on this side.

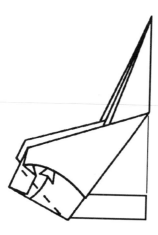

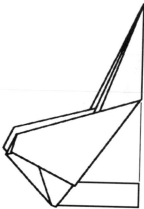

19. Repeat steps 16 and 17 for this side.

20. Both wing folds are complete.

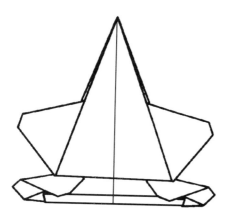

21. Flip the top wing to the right side. The paper should look like this.

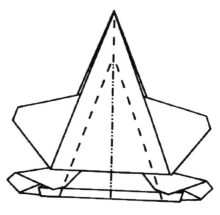

22. Approximately 1½" down from the tip, with a pivot point of about ½", make the fuselage fold. (You may need to turn the plane over to determine the pivot point from the edges of the fuselage.)

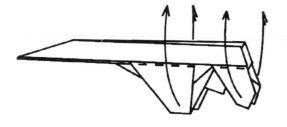

23. Fold the wings and stabilizers up on both sides.

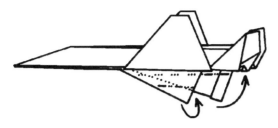

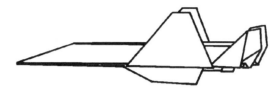

24. Reverse fold the belly up (but not the tail fin) to create a smaller belly for the plane.

25. The completed belly fold.

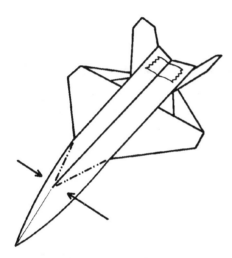

26. Tape the back of the plane and pinch the nose tightly, creating a mountain fold.

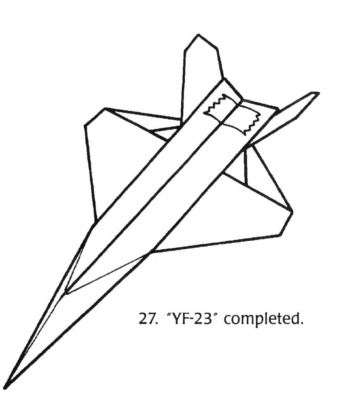

27. "YF-23" completed.

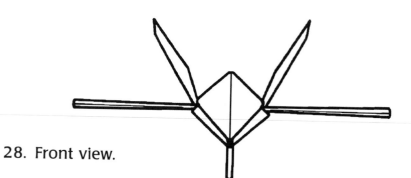

28. Front view.

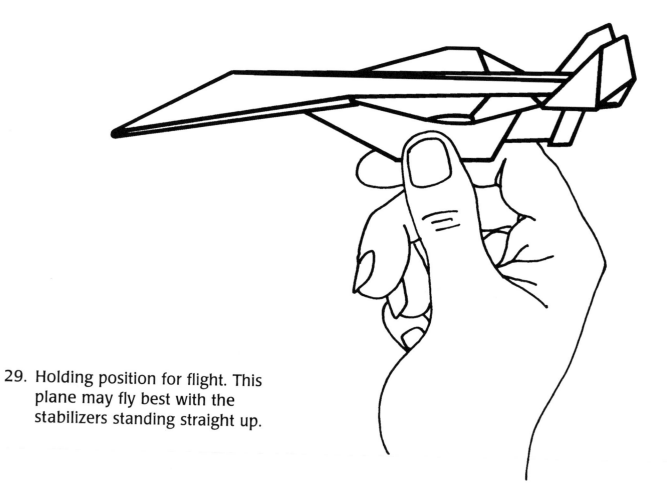

29. Holding position for flight. This plane may fly best with the stabilizers standing straight up.

16. F-5 Tiger

The F-5 was commissioned as an inexpensive fighter plane in the early '60s. The US Department of Defense sanctioned the production and sale of F-5s to allies and other favored nations. This small, lightweight plane requires a relatively short runway, allowing it to take off from a semi-prepared air strip. Powered by two General Electric J85-GE-21 engines with after-burning turbo jets that produce over 10,000 pounds of thrust, the F-5 can exceed Mach 1 at 36,000 feet.

First deployed in 1965 to Bien Hoa in South Vietnam for combat evaluation, the F-5 received excellent marks for performance and maintainability. It proved an accurate bomber and the least vulnerable fighter in the war zone. The F-5 remains a low-cost favorite among fighting aircraft, and is still in service in many nations around the globe.

Begin with Base Fold 1.

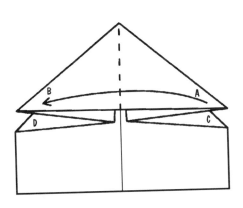

1. Fold A to the left side.

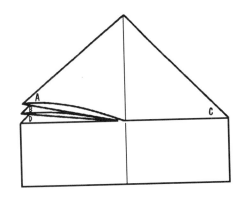

2. Your paper should look like this.

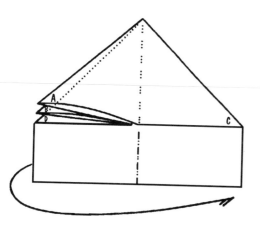

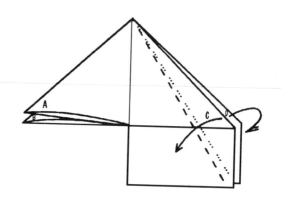

3. Flip D around the back to the right side.

4. Fold C and D in opposite directions, toward the center crease line, approximately ¼" from the fold line to the bottom right corners.

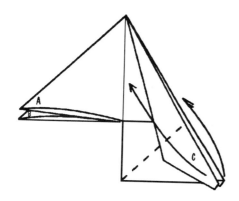

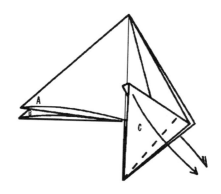

5. Fold C and D up so the bottom edges are parallel with the center crease line.

6. Fold C and D down diagonally, leaving approximately ½" at the outside edge, and pivoting down from the center crease line.

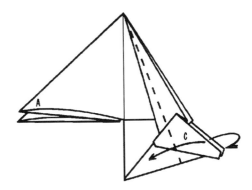

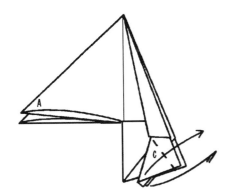

7. Fold ⅓ of C and D toward the center crease line. (Back-to-back match-fold.)

8. Fold stabilizers (C and D) out parallel to the small horizontal edge above.

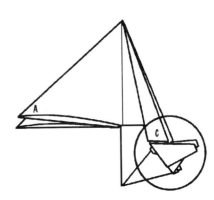

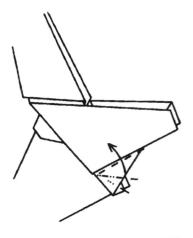

9. Focus on the stabilizers.

10. Fold the tiny web of the stabilizer up so that it will fold along with the stabilizer, as shown. It will be a squash fold (see the next diagram).

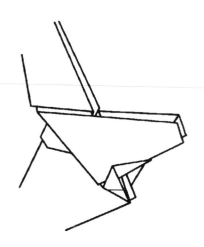

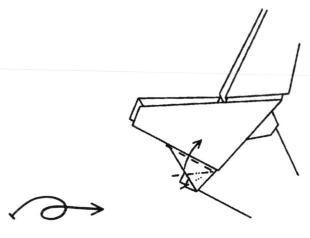

11. Completed squash fold. Turn the model over.

12. Repeat step 10 for this side.

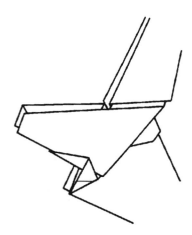

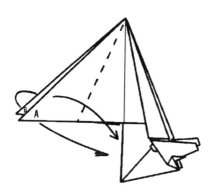

13. The completed fold.

14. Fold both wing flaps (A and B) to the center crease line in opposite directions.

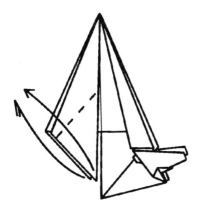

15. Approximately 2½" down from the tip, leaving ¼" at the pivot point, fold both wings (A and B) out.

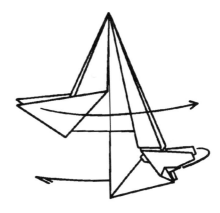

16. Flip A to the right side, and D to the left side.

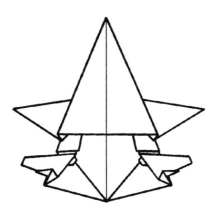

17. Your paper should look like this now.

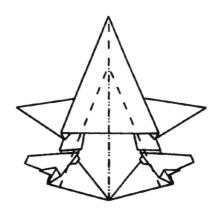

18. About 1¾" from the tip and ¼" for the pivot point, make the fuselage fold.

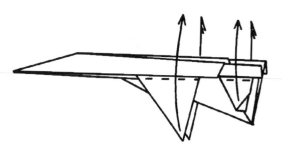

19. Fold the wings and stabilizers up.

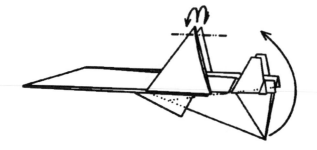

20. Reverse the tail fin up to about 1¼" high and reverse ¼" of the wing tips.

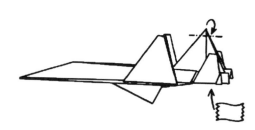

21. Tape the two inside edges under the tail fin to bond the plane. Reverse about ¼" on the tip of the tail fin.

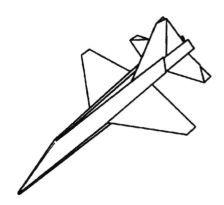

22. "F-5 Tiger" completed.

23. Bend the trailing edge of the stabilizers for lift.

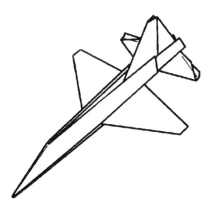

24. The plane is ready to fly.

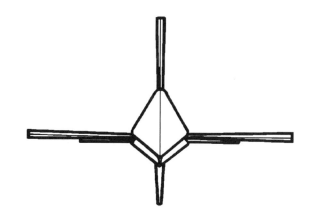

25. Front view.

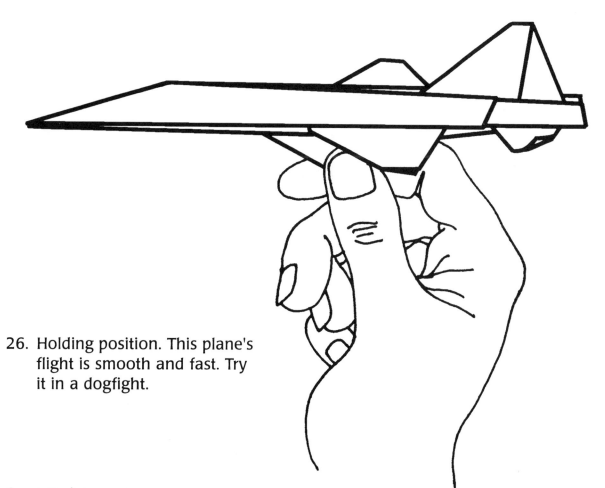

26. Holding position. This plane's flight is smooth and fast. Try it in a dogfight.

17. F-4 Phantom

The Phantom is one of the most capable and versatile of combat aircraft. Built in the early '60s, it was originally intended for strike and reconnaissance duties. Special cameras, radar and other sensors are fitted to the nose section, so the plane can gather considerable data on a single sortie. The F-4 Phantom has provided reconnaissance for several western nations, reliably gathering information from the air and sending it to the ground base.

The F-4 served as an interceptor in the British air defense from 1974 to 1980, protecting against possible intrusion from the air. With a top speed of over Mach 2, the ever-vigilant Phantom remains on duty.

Begin with Base Fold #1

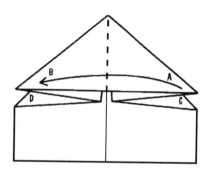

1. Flip A to the left side.

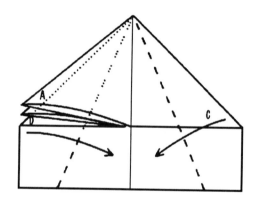

2. Fold D and C to the center crease line.

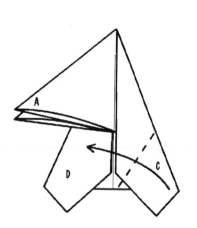

3. Fold C up diagonally so that the outside, or right edge of the fold, lies parallel with the top two flaps.

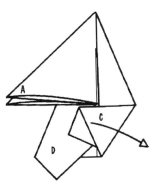

4. Unfold.

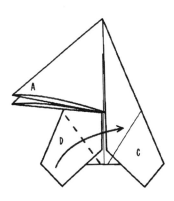

5. Repeat step 3 for flap D.

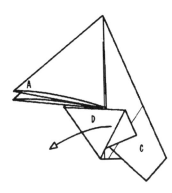

6. Unfold.

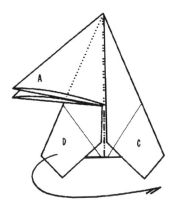

7. Flip D around the back, to the right side.

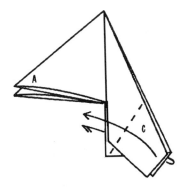

8. Fold C and D toward the center crease lines, as shown.

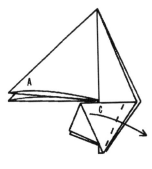

9. Fold ²/₃ of C from the center edge to the angle on the right side, pivoting down from the lower corner, as shown.

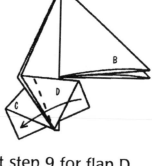

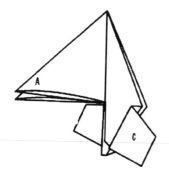

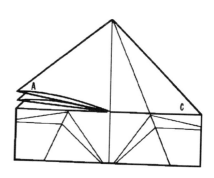

10. Turn the model over.

11. Repeat step 9 for flap D.

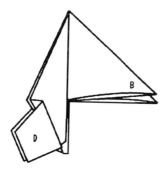

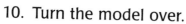

12. Unfold back to the base.

13. Turn the model over.

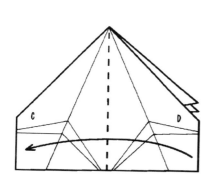

14. Flip D to the left side.

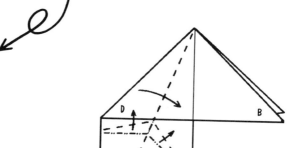

15. Now you can test your experience with the inside reverse folds you practiced at the beginning of the book. Working on flap D, make the mountain and valley folds on the creases.

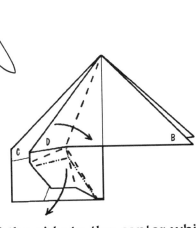

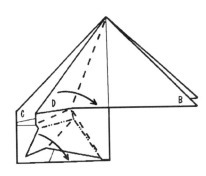

16. Fold the side to the center while pushing the bottom section of the fold out to the left side on the mountain crease lines.

17. Close the side edge to the center.

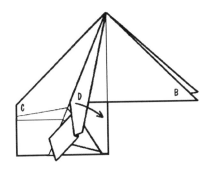

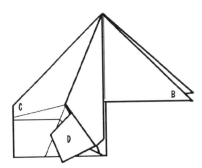

18. The folding diagram for the inside reverse fold.

19. The finished inside reverse fold. Turn over.

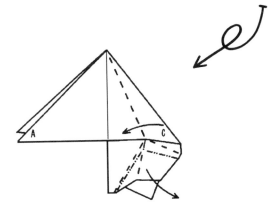

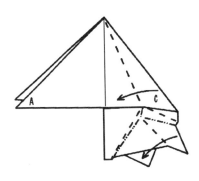

20. Working on flap C, fold the right edge to the center while mountain folding the bottom section to the right.

21. Close the side edge to the center.

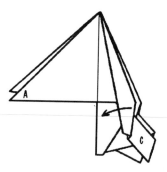

22. The folding diagram for the inside reverse fold.

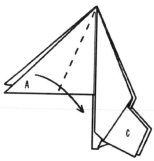

23. Fold A to the center crease line.

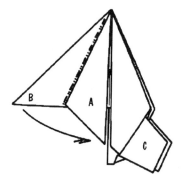

24. Mountain fold B to the center crease line.

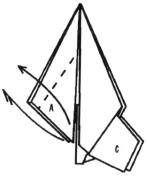

25. Approximately 2" from the tip and ¼" at the pivot point, fold both wings (A and B) out.

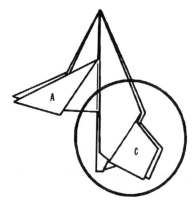

26. Focus on the circled section.

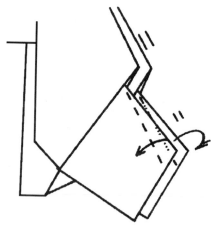

27. Make two narrow folds parallel to the above slanted edges.

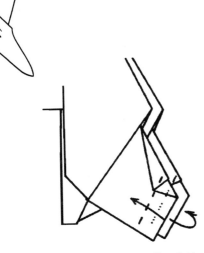

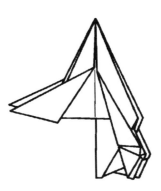

28. Fold approximately ½" of tips up diagonally.

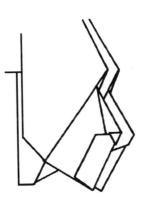

29. The folds look like this.

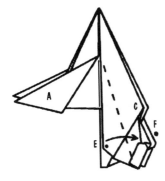

30. Fold E so it touches the small sloping edge on F. (The fold line on this step varies, so don't be concerned with differences.)

31. The fold looks like this. Turn the model over.

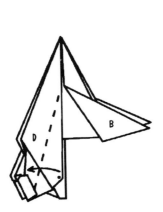

32. Repeat step 30 for flap D.

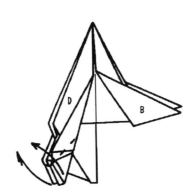

33. Fold out both stabilizers (C and D) to look like the next diagram.

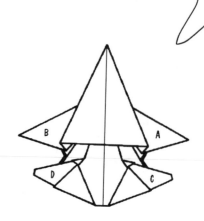

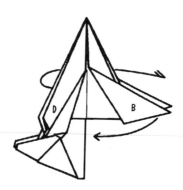

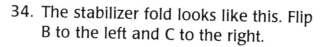

34. The stabilizer fold looks like this. Flip B to the left and C to the right.

35. Your paper should now look like this.

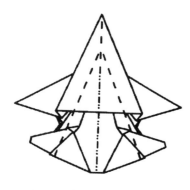

36. Approximately 1½" from the tip and 1½" from the angle of the bottom edge, make the fuselage fold.

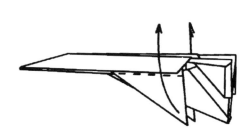

37. Fold both wings up.

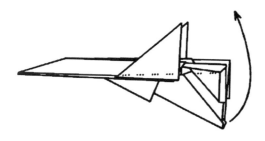

38. Reverse the tail fin up to about 1¼" high.

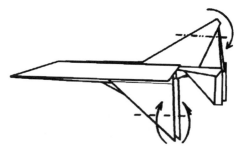

39. Reverse the tip end of the tail fin in about ½", and fold the end tip of the wings up about ¾".

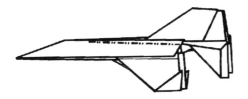

40. Carefully create this mountain fold along the back of the fuselage. (This fold will give the plane a nice flat-back fuselage, but it isn't necessary.)

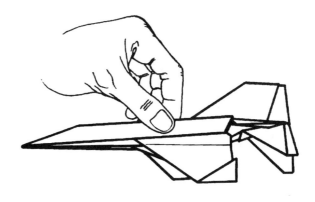

41. Pull it up like this. Turn the model over.

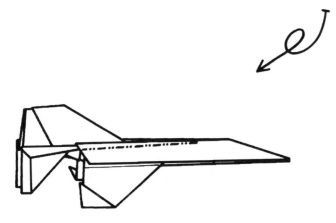

42. Repeat step 40 for this side.

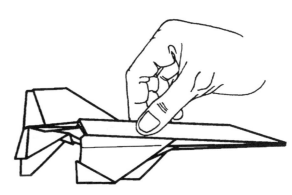

43. Pull it up.

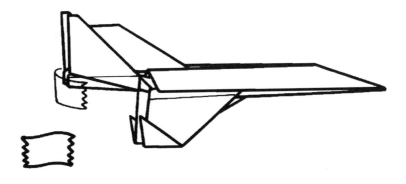

44. Tape as shown.

 Exquisite Interceptors

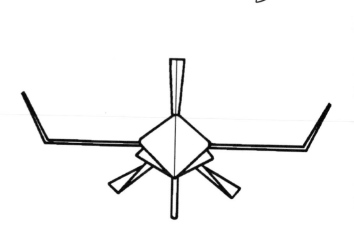

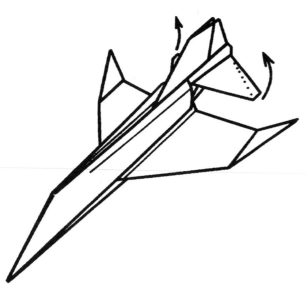

45. Trim the edges up for lift, and the plane is finished.

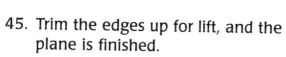

46. Front view.

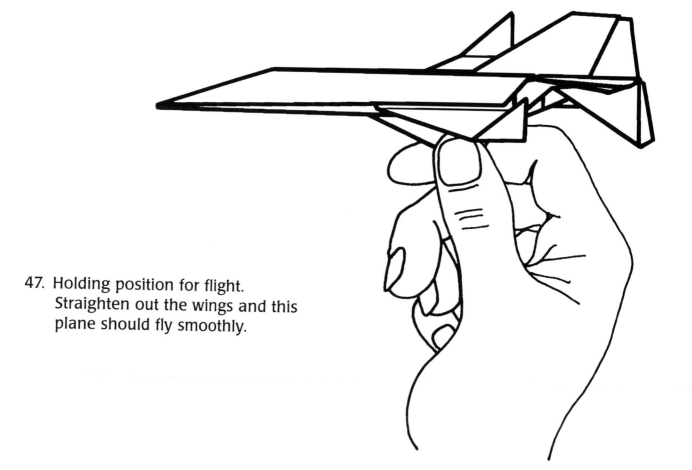

47. Holding position for flight. Straighten out the wings and this plane should fly smoothly.

About the Author

Thay Yang is an award-winning illustrator, paper airplane designer, and rocket builder. He is the author of *Exotic Paper Airplanes* (Cypress House) and co-author (with John Collins and Dan Garwood) of *Return to the Fold* (Ten Speed Press). A senior aesthetics award winner in the *Great International Paper Airplane Contest* when he was only eighteen, Thay Yang has achieved worldwide recognition as a master folder.

THE CLASSIC PAPER AIRPLANE BOOK

EXOTIC PAPER AIRPLANES

BY

THAY YANG

NEW & REVISED

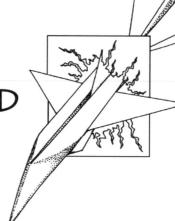

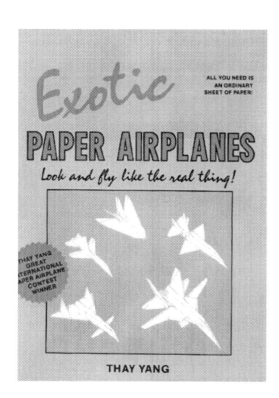

ALL YOU NEED IS AN ORDINARY SHEET OF PAPER!

Exotic PAPER AIRPLANES

Look and fly like the real thing!

THAY YANG GREAT INTERNATIONAL PAPER AIRPLANE CONTEST WINNER

THAY YANG